NATE AND BASSET, P.I.: PET INVESTIGATORS

The Mystery of the Masked Marauder

by

Peter S. Cox

For Brianna.
You inspire me to be my best and do my best.

Everything I do, I do to glorify God.

Printed in the United States of America

First Printing, 2016

ISBN 978-1514797440

www.peterscox.com

Contents

Chapter 1
MY STRANGE NEW LIFE

I talk to animals.

Other than that, my life is pretty normal.

Well talking to animals isn't that impressive; most people talk to animals. What I mean is I talk to animals, and they talk back.

Also, I'm not crazy.

Really.

Let me tell how it all started, and if you don't believe me by the end of it, that's fine. No hard feelings. I know what I know is true, and if others don't believe me then that just makes their world smaller, takes the magic out of their lives, and makes them more ignorant.

No offense.

But I think you'll believe me by the end of it. The animals helped me solve those crimes you've been reading about in the paper, and if it wasn't for them the Masked Marauder would still be on the loose.

My parents would also be dead. But I'm getting ahead of myself.

When you find out all the things I've done, all that I know, you'll see that talking animals is the *only* thing that makes sense.

It all started last year, just a few days after my 13th birthday. I was walking home from school on the last day before summer vacation, in a pretty bad mood (I'll tell you more about that in a minute), and had just entered my fenced-in backyard when my dog Basset came running out of the back door towards me.

That's nothing unusual.

What *was* unusual was how he greeted me.

With words.

"Buddy, buddy, hey buddy," I heard a voice pant out, like someone was way too excited. "You're finally home and I wasn't sure if you were coming back or not and there was a neat smell earlier that you should smell and I'm glad you're home," the voice said in one long run-on sentence.

I stopped and stared.

The voice was coming from my dog.

Obviously, I thought I was crazy.

In most movies or stories, people pinch themselves to see if they're dreaming. I didn't. Because that's stupid. First off, have you ever, and I mean ever, had a dream that actually felt real? Whenever I'm dreaming, everything seems off, time doesn't move like it should, and the plot keeps jumping around randomly.

Also, I'm usually in my underwear.

Second, how would pinching yourself tell you that you're awake? Is pinching the one thing that's impossible to dream about? Running away from a flying ketchup monster through the halls of my school at night while one of my teachers sings karaoke, *that's* possible; but pinching yourself is just too much?

Makes no sense.

So I figured I was either going crazy (and mostly there), or someone was playing a trick on me. When he talked, Basset's mouth didn't move like in most talking dog movies (with terrible animation), so I figured it could be a walkie-talkie hidden nearby

2

somewhere.

Either way, I decided to go with it. If it was a joke, it was a good one, and I might as well give everyone a laugh. And if I was going crazy, why not start talking to the dog? That sounds like a fun kind of crazy to me.

"Is that you boy?" I asked, hesitantly. "Are…are you talking to me?" I reached a shaking hand out to pet him as he sat at my feet, panting away.

Basset closed his mouth, stopped panting, and looked up at me with a serious expression on his face. He's a golden retriever, so he can get that solemn, almost sad look on his face sometimes, like he's deep in thought, but it's rare, and never when he's first greeting me.

"It's me," I heard the voice say slowly. "But does that mean…you can hear me?"

"I can hear you…" I said, trailing off myself, not sure what to say next.

Then it hit me: a way to figure out if this was a trick after all.

"Basset, what do I do every night, right before bedtime prayers?"

"You tell me about your day, of course," he said.

That settled it. None of the other kids in the neighborhood could possibly know about that.

So I was either insane, or this was real.

"But how can you hear me?" Basset asked. "You've never been able to hear me before."

"The real question is how can you *talk*?"

"I've always been able to talk." He sighed, like he was having trouble explaining something. "We can all talk. All the animals I mean. Well not all…it's tough to describe. Anyway, we can talk to each other, but humans have never been able to hear us

3

. . . until now."

I stood still for a second, too stunned to move. Let me tell you, learning that all the animals in the world are thinking, talking creatures and you have a gift no one else on earth has… well, it's a lot to absorb.

Or I could have been insane. That's a lot to absorb too.

"But then why were you talking, just now when you were running up to me?"

"Why do you humans talk to us when you think *we* can't respond?"

"Fair enough," I said with a smile. "Fair enough."

I paused.

"Well this puts a new spin on our friendship."

"I'd say so," he panted. "A good spin though, right?"

"Oh, definitely," I smiled. "Definitely a good spin."

I led him inside then, slightly dazed. Now it felt kind of like I really was in a dream, my head all foggy like when you have a bad fever or haven't slept in days.

My parents weren't home from work yet and I'm an only child, so we had the house to ourselves like we do most days.

My parents' house isn't anything special: a three bedroom Cape Cod-style place on a quiet street with a big, shady backyard for Basset and me. It's nice having all that room to run around and play fetch, and it's great having my own room, but my one complaint is that we only have one bathroom. It can get crazy in the mornings when we're all getting ready at the same time.

Anyway, we went upstairs to my bedroom. It's a little small and cramped, but it's perfect for me: it's cozy, quiet, and a perfect place to read, which is my favorite thing to do besides playing with Basset. On the walls were posters of some of my favorite bands (Muse, mostly), and I had fantasy books scattered everywhere. Of course, if I really did have a talking dog, I figured I'd have a little less interest in fantastical stories.

I plopped down on my bed, and Basset followed me up as he had done thousands of times before, and sat there looking at me with that stupid, openmouthed panting grin golden retrievers love to give.

It seemed so normal I almost started to think that everything had just been a daydream.

Then Basset started talking again.

"What do we do now I mean now that we can talk to each other and do you think it will last or will it stop just as suddenly as it started?"

"Don't ask ME," I said with a slight laugh.

"But what are we gonna do now to find out?"

"I guess… maybe just give me a moment. I need a minute to process this; a talking dog is just too weird."

"Same for me. You think a talking dog is weird? That's my life every day. But a listening human? Now *that's* weird."

I sat for a minute, trying to figure out exactly *how* to process something like this. I always heard people say stuff like that in movies, but I didn't know how they did it.

"Hey," I said slowly, "why do you talk like that sometimes?"

"Like what?" he asked cautiously.

"Well most of the time you talk normally, or I guess I mean like a normal *human*, I have no idea what's normal for a dog, but then sometimes you talk really fast and kind of running on like the words just start flowing out of your head all at once and you can't even keep up."

"Oh, that," he sounded slightly embarrassed. "I try not to do that, but sometimes I just get too excited, and everything comes out all at once. It's relatively common for dogs, I think."

I'd soon learn just how right he was.

Dogs are a pretty excitable bunch.

Even if you can't hear *what* they're saying to you, most people probably know that.

Basset was different than most other dogs though. I think it's because he's a golden retriever. They seem to have more patience and wisdom than most dogs. But they can still get carried away sometimes.

"Well if we can't figure out *why* we can talk to each other, then I guess we can't figure out how to keep it from going away," I said. "Assuming you don't want it to go away."

"Are you kidding buddy this is awesome just about the best thing ever I mean we can finally talk to each other."

I laughed. "There you go again." You can't see a dog blush of course, but you can sure tell when he is embarrassed. And I swear he was blushing under all that fur.

"Sorry, boy. I was just teasing. It's fun when you get that excited."

He slowed down, but he overdid it a little, pausing between each word like when you're trying to talk to someone who speaks a different language. "Wellllll, you're riiight. We should juuuust go with it for now, and hope it doesn't goooo away. I've alwaaaays wished I could taaaalk to you, but never thooought it would be possible."

"Me too. Me too."

We sat looking at each other for a couple of minutes in silence, both of us just thinking. Then something hit me.

"Hey! Do you think I can talk to other animals too?"

He paused. "Probably. I mean, I have no idea how this works, but tomorrow I can take you around and introduce you to some of my friends and we'll see what happens."

"Cool."

My parents were bound to get home from work soon, and

I really wasn't sure what I should do when they did.

"What do you think, Basset? Should I tell my parents about all this?"

"Hmmmm…" Even though a dog can't really close his lips and make a humming noise, that's what I heard from Basset. It made sense: he doesn't *use* his lips to talk to me. Like I said, when he talks it doesn't look like bad animation, I just hear it. Not in my head, either, like if it was telepathy, but with my ears. I don't know how it works; I'm not an Animal-Human-Telepathic-Communication Expert. Also, I'm pretty sure there's no such thing as an Animal-Human-Telepathic-Communication Expert.

At least I hope not.

"I'm not sure telling your parents is a good idea," he continued. "I mean, I can try to talk to your parents to see if *everyone* can suddenly hear animals, but my guess is that won't work. And if they can't hear me, you shouldn't say anything to them about it. They'll probably think you're crazy."

"That's what I figured," I said with a sigh. "To be honest, I think I'm probably crazy," I chuckled.

"Well I can tell you that you aren't crazy, but I'm not sure that would help. The figment of your imagination telling you it isn't a figment of your imagination doesn't really prove anything."

I really hate keeping secrets from my parents. They're decent enough, and I try not to lie to them if I can help it. We're not best friends or anything, but they're fine. They can be busy at work and sometimes ignore me, but that's normal.

I did have one secret already, though, something that I only told Basset because it's not like he could tell anyone. Or at least that's what I thought until today.

I was having trouble with bullies.

Chapter 2
DECIDING WHAT TO DO

It's embarrassing, but it's true. I was kind of short and scrawny for my age, so I guess I was pretty easy to push around.

It's not like they show in the movies. You know how it is in real life: I didn't get beat up, or get a swirly in the toilet or anything. Nothing so drastic. But a couple of bigger kids – led by a particularly tall monster of a boy named Guster who had terrible acne and breath like sauerkraut – always *threatened* to beat me up. I was never sure if they'd really do that, and risk me having physical proof that they were bugging me, but I didn't want to risk it. They threatened until I gave them my lunch money, which I always did.

I asked my parents to pack me a homemade lunch once, but just that once. Guster took my ham sandwich, dunked it in the toilet, and then gave it back to me. I guess he didn't want my lunch money to buy lunch. He then smashed my Star Trek lunchbox. I told my parents I dropped it during my walk to school.

I know some states have anti-bully laws, and all the schools have anti-bully programs and anti-bully assemblies and anti-bully everything, but that doesn't always work. Anti-bully reporting only works if teachers *see* someone bullying. And anti-bullying assemblies and classes only work if bullies happen to be nice, intelligent people who pay attention in class and will listen to appeals to their better nature, which just happens to be the exact opposite of what a bully is. It's kind of in the job description.

I wanted to tell my parents or tell a teacher, I really did, but I was too scared. Scared that the bully would get punished, and then he'd punish *me* for some nice cold revenge. Bullies aren't the most creative bunch, but I didn't really want to encourage them to try coming up with a creative punishment.

Honestly, I was most scared of becoming a tattletale. I know that sounds ridiculous, but things weren't going well for me when it came to making friends, and I didn't want to make it any worse. That was my biggest fear.

We had moved to Grant County just a couple weeks ago, coming from across the country. It was an easy move for my parents, one quiet neighborhood to another, one job to a slightly better one, but for me it was hard. Really hard.

I didn't have any close friends back in my old school, but I had a couple of guys that I would hang out with. We'd play video games or go to the park to play fetch with Basset or something. But here it seemed impossible to find anyone. Everyone seemed to already be in their own little group, and none of them were looking for new members.

It didn't help that a lot of kids teased me.

It's never about anything major. I'm small, so some kids call me pipsqueak or other, meaner names about my size. My first day at my new school I didn't know that sweaters were "wicked uncool," and I wore a really baggy sweater that my dad had given me from one of my older cousins.

The "grandma sweater" – as the other kids called it – was just the start. My parents never had a lot of money, even though they both worked, so a lot of my clothes were hand-me-downs. Usually really dated, out of style hand-me-downs.

I didn't have bell bottoms or flowery, frilly shirts, but I had a lot of grungy stuff from the 90s. No one wanted to hang out with the "grunge" kid. Even if I thought Nirvana was a toneless, whiny band with loud guitars, my *clothes* said I liked grunge.

And that was enough.

I also had a different accent from the other kids, and everything I said seemed to make them laugh.

Like when I called it a "water fountain" instead of a "bubbler" and they all called me an idiot.

I never used to be shy at my old school; I liked to be funny and sarcastic sometimes, and never hesitated to speak up. But after a couple days of everything I said or did being wrong, I just clammed up. I hardly ever spoke in school anymore unless I was called on.

It's hard to make friends when you don't talk to anyone.

The only thing that I could rely on, the only constant that stayed the same from my old life, was Basset. He was there for me all the time, no matter what I wore or what I did. Sometimes it seemed lame to have an animal as a best friend because he couldn't talk back to me, but he still made me feel a lot less lonely at night when I'd see pictures on Facebook of people from school hanging out at the mall or going to concerts.

Now that he could talk, I felt a *lot* less lonely. But as I sat there thinking, I still wished I had a best friend, someone I could tell about all this. Someone *human*.

At that moment my parents came home (they always carpooled to save money), with a loud bang from a car door, followed by another, even louder bang.

They were probably fighting again.

They did that a lot now.

"Nate, we're home!" I heard my mom shout up the stairs, as if they had snuck into the house instead using the car doors like their own personal drum kit. "We brought home pizza for dinner!"

"We'll talk more about this later," I whispered to Basset as I ran downstairs.

We always had dinner together, even if it was just takeout or fast food.

The whole time we were eating, I tried my hardest to seem normal. You know how it is: the harder I tried to look normal, the more I started to doubt what normal was.

Am I eating too fast? Wait, now I'm eating in slow motion like it's the lamest action-movie-pizza-eating scene ever. Am I not meeting my parents' eyes when they ask me about my day? Or am I staring into their eyes *too* much? I feel like this is a creepy amount of eye-staring.

Mostly I just tried to keep out of sight. You can't usually hide at a normal dinner table, but we had a massive lamp sitting in the middle of our table; an ornate, extremely fancy globe light covered in frilly, lace-like etchings.

It looked like it belonged in a Victorian house, not on a cheap Ikea table used to eat pizza.

The lamp had been sitting in the basement of the house when we moved in, forgotten by the old owners. My mom called it "the most hideous thing I've seen outside my grandmother's house," but my dad insisted on keeping it and putting it on display.

He said it classed up the house.

It made me feel like I was in a nursing home.

Which is not a particularly classy feeling.

But today I loved that lamp. I hid behind the stark orange globe the size of my head for most of the meal. Hard to have a conversation with a giant glowing ball in front of your face.

My parents never seemed to notice. Either they were too distracted by their own thoughts and anxieties, or I was a really good actor and didn't even know it.

My guess is that it was the first one.

11

Basset did come downstairs at one point and said hello, but my parents didn't even flinch. From their perspective there must have been absolutely no sound.

One of my theories had been that maybe I had learned to understand Basset's barks, like how some people can learn Spanish just by being around a lot of Mexican people. But that clearly wasn't the case here.

After that, Basset gave me a sad look, and went back upstairs.

It was a painfully slow dinner, partly because of how hard I was working to seem normal and how scared I was that they'd know I was keeping a secret, and partly because I couldn't wait to go upstairs and talk to Basset more.

There was a whole other world out there, a world of talking animals. Imagine all the things they could tell me, all the things I could discover!

The wait was killing me.

It didn't help that half the words out of my parents' mouths were jabs at each other.

"So taking out the trash later?" "I told you I'd get around to it. I'll get around to it."

I figured it had to do with the stress of moving and finding new jobs and not having enough money, but I still wished they could work these things out *together* instead of against each other. But what do I know, I'm just a kid.

I won't write about any of the specifics here, because it doesn't really matter, does it? It never changes from house to house, really. They fought about how to spend money, usually when one of them wanted to buy something the other thought was "frivolous," or about how to spend the little free time they had on the weekends. But usually it wasn't about anything. When people get stressed, they snap at each other over little things, and then the person who gets snapped at is also stressed, so they snap back. In my house there was more snapping going around than at a snap-clasp factory.

That was a stupid analogy. Sorry.

Once dinner was over, my plan was to sprint right up the stairs as fast as I could.

"After you're done eating, I'll help you with your math homework," my dad said. "Then we'll have some family time."

So much for that idea.

My parents always insisted on doing "family time" every few nights. It was usually just us sitting and watching a movie or some TV together, which fits the "together" part of "family togetherness" but I never understood how it made us any more of a family.

How does silently watching something in the same room as someone else count as quality time?

"Hey kids, let's sit in the same room and not talk to each other for a few hours! It will be almost like sleeping in the same room, except we'll be awake!"

They had rented that animated movie about the talking rhinoceros who does karate to fight the evil penguins. You know the one.

It didn't really hold my attention. Not when there was a *real* talking animal sitting up in my room waiting for me.

Not doing karate, but still.

Basset came down once or twice, but he never seemed interested in movies before, and this time was no different. He'd come in, I'd smile at him, he'd watch the movie for a couple seconds, and then pad out of the room silently.

When it was time for bed, I knew I wouldn't have a chance to talk to Basset. My parents had caught me staying up late to read enough times to get tired of it, and they now checked on me regularly to make sure I was quiet and my lights were off.

"Goodnight buddy," I whispered as I climbed under the covers. "We'll have to chat some more tomorrow."

"Okay," he whispered back.

"Why are you whispering? I'm the only one who can hear you."

"I'm not sure," he said, again in a whisper. "Just seems like the right thing to do so late at night. Besides, I think there's a squirrel outside, and I don't want to spook it."

"Ah," I said, reminding myself to ask him some questions tomorrow about how the animals all get along with each other. "Well, goodnight."

"Goodnight, buddy," he said back.

He curled up at the foot of my bed, like he had every night, then we drifted off to sleep.

And that's when the face appeared at my window.

Chapter 3
THE MASKED PHANTOM

In the middle of the night I woke up in a cold sweat, bolting upright in bed. I didn't know what it was, but something had me spooked. Basset was nowhere in sight, and my heart was pounding away like I had run a race, or was face-to-prematurely-pimply-face with Guster. It was weird, but I felt scared, like someone was watching me.

I turned to look out the window, and felt a nasty icy pit form in my stomach.

Someone *was* watching me.

Right at the glass of the window a masked face with blank, hollow eyes was staring in at me. It looked like the mask from that Phantom of the Opera movie my mom loved so much, except that it covered the whole face instead of just half of it: it was icy white and inhuman, like a death mask. It was pitch dark outside, and all I could see was the death-white face. No clothes, no body, nothing but the eyeless face floating in the darkness, staring right at me.

I wanted to run away, spring into my parents' room as fast as I could, but I was too scared. I was scared that if I moved one inch, even flinched, the face outside would see me, and would burst through the window with a crash and come right at me.

So I sat there, sweating more icy bullets.

15

Slowly, a white glove appeared in the window, it also appearing to float in midair.

The window had a thin film of pollen stuck to it, and the gloved hand went straight for the glass and started to write in the dust.

It didn't make a sound, but within seconds it had spelled out "Death is coming. Look in Baskertonn Manor." Then the other hand came up to the window and wrote "2 1 19 20 15 14."

It was an ambidextrous phantom, apparently.

I had no idea what the writing meant. I had overheard some of the other kids at school talk about the old Baskertonn place. It was supposed to be buried back in the woods somewhere, an old abandoned house that no one had lived in in over a hundred years. There were all sorts of stories about the place – ghosts and witches and nonsense like that – but none of the kids knew much for sure about the manor. No one had seen it in 50 years, they said. Even their parents didn't know where it was, but everyone knew it was real.

That was the story at least.

So I knew what that part meant, but the rest of it was just…weird.

Suddenly, I blinked and the face was gone, the window was back to normal, and Basset was back at the foot of my bed, sound asleep.

It had been a nightmare.

It took me a while to fall back asleep, but when I finally did the memory of that nightmare slowly faded away, until I didn't remember it at all.

When I woke up, Basset was just stirring at the foot of the bed, and he looked up at me.

"Morning boy," I said, a flutter of excitement playing in my stomach as I thought of all the things I would do and learn today.

There was no response.

Chapter 4
MEETING THE ANIMALS

"Boy?" I asked, hesitantly.

Still nothing.

Had it all been a dream?

Of course it had. I had been stupid – incredibly stupid – to think that the day before could have been real. Talking dogs? Who's seriously gullible or lonely or desperate enough to believe that? It's ridiculous.

I was disappointed, of course, because that dream gave me a glimpse of a different life, of escape from a life without friends. Even more, it meant that the world of adults – the world that was always reasonable, the world that told us Santa wasn't real and aliens are only in movies and everything is neat and ordered and there are no more surprises, the world of bills and working until you're too stressed to enjoy your money – was *wrong*.

Sorry for that last sentence, sometimes my thoughts can be a bit like a dog's, I guess: excitable.

The dream told me there was still some mystery out there, some wonderful things to discover and explore.

So yeah, I was disappointed.

But I have to admit I was relieved too.

Getting to live out some adventures in a magical world

might seem exciting in a story. Not so much when it's real.

Talking animals would mean even more people to get to know, more rules for being polite, and who knew what was going on out there? Were some animals at war with others? Would some of the animals be dangerous knowing that I could hear them? Would the government come after me?

You know how difficult it is to start going to a new school in a new town. Well, imagine that not only do you not know the teachers or the students and you're all alone, you don't know *anything* and you're all alone. You don't know any of the rules: You don't know how your life works anymore, what words will get your head lopped off by some disgruntled grizzly bear, or which animals are friendly and furry, and which creatures are little balls of nasty.

It would be a tad overwhelming.

But if you asked me right then and there, I would have said my disappointment outweighed my relief. In other words, I would rather the dream be real. I would rather face the danger and the mystery and the enormity of a new world than go back to my old life.

Which is good.

Because it *was* real.

As I was thinking all this and wrestling with these thoughts, I heard a cough, then a sputter.

"Hack! Gruffffff. Blech. Sorry buddy, something caught in my throat. I ate some brown stuff in the backyard last night and it's not really agreeing with me this morning."

"Bas-set!" I almost screamed the first part of his name I was so excited, then remembered that I had to keep quiet, and quickly whispered the second part. It sounded like someone switched on the TV with it way too loud, then quickly turned it back down.

"I thought for a second it was all a dream!" I whispered

back.

"I'm so sorry to scare you," he said, giving me that sad look he was so good at. "Brown stuff, you know."

I smiled. "Why DO you dogs eat things when you have no idea what they are?"

"I don't know," he said slowly, like he had never even thought of it before. "Why do humans *not* eat random stuff? Who knows what you're missing out on!"

I laughed. "I guess you're right. But I still think I'll skip the brown stuff, thanks just the same."

"I think that's a good idea. It wasn't great."

He shook his head a couple of times, like he was trying to shake the taste away, and then turned back to me with his mouth hanging open, the smile I had seen a thousand times on his face, like when he knows it's time to go outside for a walk or some fetch.

"So what do you want to do first?" he asked haltingly, like he was trying to talk slowly, but wasn't quite getting it. "There's a lot of stuff I've wanted to tell you for a long time now and I never thought I'd be able to and now I can and I don't even know where to start but I also want to take you around the neighborhood and see if you can understand everyone and introduce you to some other dogs and maybe a few of the nicer cats and – "

I laughed, and Basset got that look like he was blushing under his fur again.

"Sorry, buddy," he said. "Got carried away again."

"It's okay boy," I said, giving him a quick hug. "I understand. I'm excited too. Let me get dressed and get some breakfast, then we can head out around town. I want to talk to you too, but Mom and Dad would think it's weird if I stayed in my room all morning on the first day of summer break!"

He nodded his head and his smile widened. He loved going

outside.

"Hey, that reminds me," I said. "I know we can't understand you when you talk, but if you animals are all... I don't know.... smart? .... Well, how come you never try to communicate with us in other ways? Like nodding your head?"

"Would *you* think a dog was nodding its head at you, or would you think you were going crazy?" I nodded MY head. "It's best not to even try. It causes too much trouble. People think they're seeing things, or think their dog is crazy. Some dogs have tried it. It... never ends well." He had a tone in his voice that told me he didn't want to talk about it anymore. I didn't know what that was all about, but I didn't want to make him upset. He seemed sad talking about it. Lonely, almost.

As we were heading downstairs for breakfast, I thought I heard a scuffling noise coming from the crawlspace door. I turned and looked, and hesitated.

When my parents first bought this old house, they moved a rickety bookcase on the landing to find a tiny, crooked door that they figured must lead into a crawlspace. It was only about three feet high, but it was locked tight with three bulky padlocks.

My dad kept saying he wanted to get a locksmith in here to get that door open and see what was inside. My mom said it was probably just some musty old Christmas decorations too tacky to use, but Dad said you never know, there could be old baseball cards in there or something.

So far they still hadn't gotten around to getting the door open.

The noise freaked me out a little, but I figured it was nothing but a mouse back there. One of the locks looked like it was open, and I wanted to test the others and see if I could go explore in there myself, but before I could my dad suddenly came to the bottom of the stairs.

Just as suddenly, the noise stopped.

After a rushed breakfast with my parents (my mom had some work to get done, even though it was a Saturday, and my dad had a lot of house projects to work on), they asked me what I'd be up to all day.

"Just exploring around town a bit," I told them.

They seemed happy about that, but my mom of course asked "Meeting up with any friends?" to which I just shook my head, a little sadly.

Then Basset and I ran out the back door, and into "the unknown."

I love to explore. In my old town some of the guys and I would head back into the woods that were behind my parents' house and just wander.

I always loved following unknown paths in the woods, especially ones overgrown and untouched for years, ones that barely counted as a path at all.

Chances are paths in the suburbs will lead you to accidentally trespassing in someone else's yard and then lead you to some serious grounding (that only happened to me twice), or they'll lead you to something as exciting as an alley behind a convenience store. I knew that. But I still held out hope that one of these paths would lead to some unexplored corner of the world that people hadn't seen in years.

You might think that's ridiculous. Most people do. But maybe that's why it's possible, because everyone thinks it's impossible. I mean, if no one explores these paths because they're too boring, doesn't that just make it more likely that the end of them is unexplored?

I guess I like to daydream.

In my old town we found old train tracks that hadn't been used in so long people forgot they were there, and weeds and small trees were growing between the ties. We found streams to fish in that no one else knew about, and small caves full of rocks that looked like Indian arrowheads and old bottles from hundreds of years ago with cool labels for products that no one alive had heard of (my favorites were "Dr. Johnson's Magical Healing Fish Oil" and "Mushroom Tonic"). And best of all there were shortcuts to different areas of town. We could get from school to the library so fast it was like we had a secret passageway, and we got our hands on the new Harry Potter books before any of the other kids could even get halfway to the library.

They were pretty jealous, which just made it even more fun.

Like I said, this neighborhood wasn't much different from the one that we had left, at least on the surface of things. There was a massive wooded lot behind our house, and I had no idea how far back it went. I looked forward to exploring back there and seeing all the mysteries it was hiding.

I had already found a couple of forgotten places: an old empty freight train compartment rusting away in the woods, a few small caves, and a stone wall that seemed to be in the middle of nowhere.

There were more houses lining my street on both sides, like your standard quiet suburb. Some of the houses had kids, some didn't. There was only one abandoned house on the street, the old Johnson place, and I had been strictly forbidden from ever going near it. It had been "condemned" and was apparently a really dangerous place to play, because the roof could give in at any moment, and there was shattered glass all around.

"So where should we go first?" I asked, whispering and looking back at the house to make sure no one saw me talking to the dog.

"Well we can go meet Douglas, the hound next door. He's

old and a little slow, but he's a nice old fella. Or we can see Genevieve, the cat a block from here. She knows all the local gossip and can tell you a lot about the animals in the neighborhood."

"I thought dogs and cats don't get along," I said with a smirk.

"It's never good to generalize, buddy," he said. "But that's true: *most* cats are terrible."

"What do you mean?" I asked, looking forward to getting an answer to one of mankind's oldest mysteries: why dogs and cats fight.

"Most of them are stuck up, self-centered snobs," he said with disgust. "Not anywhere near as friendly as us dogs. But they'll tell you they're more 'cultured' which is just another word for 'snobby.'"

"Probably because they don't go around eating 'brown stuff,'" I laughed.

Basset knew me well enough not to get upset. He knew I was kidding.

"Probably," he laughed.

That really wasn't the great revelation to the mystery I had hoped for. I mean, everyone knows that about cats, right?

At that moment I heard some chattering from the woods, and noticed a small group of squirrels looking our way.

"What about them?" I asked, motioning to the little pack. "Want to introduce me to the squirrels?"

"Ummm..." he hesitated. "I'd rather not. We don't... get along real well."

"What do you mean?"

"Well... squirrels tend to be - kind of - jerks. They like to tease dogs because we're slower and can't climb trees. I have to admit, I don't respond well to that. If they annoy me, I like to *chase* them up the trees. They hate that, which makes me a little happier."

"I thought you said not to generalize," I laughed.

"With squirrels it's okay." He paused. "Who knows, maybe some of them are nice. But not the ones around here. Around here they're jerks."

The next couple of days were a whirlwind of meeting new friends, discovering new places, and learning about a whole new world.

This would be a good time to clear up some misconceptions about talking animals from those terribly unrealistic kids' movies.

For one thing, in movies and books animals usually have "typical" animal names like "Squirrelly the Squirrel" or "Fred Fish." That's stupid. How many times do you run into a classmate named "Boy-y the Boy" or "Gilly Girl." Most of my animal friends have normal names, like Rex or Fido or Franklin or Peter. I did once meet a cow named Lucretia. That's pretty weird. But usually the names are normal.

Also, animals are like people in a lot of ways. Like Basset said, you can't assume anything about an animal just because of his species. Sure, squirrels talk really fast and dogs can get overly excited and cats can be *really* snooty, but assuming a pit-bull is mean just because he's a pit-bull would be just as bad as... well, something racist. We don't have to go there.

The point is, you don't want to be a specist. Or speciesist. Whatever you'd call it. The species are all different in their own ways, and each culture has some definite characteristics, but you can't *assume* anything. Not ever.

Some animals are nice, and some animals are mean.

For instance, a two ton gorilla wearing an eye patch and a tutu with a really bad attitude once tried to pack me into a suitcase far too small for me to fit in because I foiled his diamond heist plan.

That's another story, but it illustrates my point well: animals can be just as hard to get along with as people.

Chapter 5
GOSSIP

On the third night of summer vacation, Basset finally got the chance to tell me what he'd been waiting to say.

"Listen buddy," he said slowly while he was curled up at the foot of my bed. From his tone of voice I could tell he was going to tell me something important.

I had honestly been dreading this moment.

I was scared to hear what Basset had to say to me.

Basically, I was scared it would be bad advice. And that would make him wrong, which would make him....normal.

My whole life Basset had been my confidant. He'd always listened to everything I had to say, with the same content look on his face. He'd been by my side through everything.

Now that he could talk, everything that I suspected about my golden retriever had so far been proven true: he was thoughtful, patient, and downright wise.

But if he gave the same advice as my parents, wouldn't that make him just as wise as my parents?

No offense to them, but their advice was terrible.

"I know you've been lonely since we've moved to town," Basset said. "I've been lonely too, trust me. You couldn't understand me speak, while I could understand you, so I didn't

27

have to live with silence. But I didn't have anyone to talk to."

"You do now buddy."

"I know. And nothing has made me happier. But I want to tell you I think it will get better. If you pay attention to which kids are teasing you, I'm sure you'll find a few who aren't so mean. And if you're brave enough, maybe they can be your friends. Not all the kids can be terrible, right?"

"It sure seems like it sometimes."

"I know, but I think there are some good ones. You just have to find them."

I nodded.

"But until then, you have me."

He smiled at me, but I still noticed a sad look in his eyes.

It was a lot better than the advice my parents gave me, which was always the same, and is probably the exact same advice your parents give you.

"Someday you'll grow up, and realize that being popular in school didn't really matter." Or "someday you'll grow up, and see that this wasn't really a big deal."

Do parents really forget that much about being our age? "Someday it will be different," isn't super helpful for today. Today is not someday. It's today. That's why it's called "today."

Imagine if I tried to give that advice to my parents. "Don't worry Dad, someday you won't even remember what you were fighting with Mom about, so it doesn't really matter who wins." Or "someday you'll realize that impressing your boss wasn't really that important."

It IS important right now, because guess what, right now IS right now, and what matters now matters now because now is now. Make sense?

I think they just tell us that because they don't have better advice to give. At least not off the top of their heads, and they can't be bothered to sit and think about a solution to our problems.

I have no friends. I'm not happy. If you can't help me make friends, at least offer me a little understanding, or some comfort or *something*. Not "it doesn't matter."

By telling us that what we care about won't matter to our adult selves, doesn't that mean that *we* don't matter? Because what we care about is a big part of who we *are*.

Basset's advice was way better. Especially because it came with some comfort. And a good amount of thought, effort, and understanding.

***

The next morning my mom had one of her neighborhood friends over – a Mrs. Maplewood – and wanted me to sit down and visit.

It was a disaster.

Mrs. Maplewood was an interior decorator who talked faster than those guys at the ends of car commercials on the radio. And it was always about something boring.

My mom couldn't get enough.

"So how's school going, Nate?" she asked me when I sat down.

"Okay, I guess. We're out for summer now."

"Oh my, how fun! You know, I was just saying to Elvira Smith that summer is my favorite time of year, because the decorating colors are all bright and sunny. You know, you really should take more care to switch out your drapes and curtains with the seasons, my dear," she said to my mom.

Funny how "how's school" turned into "look how fancy I am, let me talk a billion miles per hour about it."

She just kept going. "And flowers are an integral part of

your decorating."

"Yes, I was thinking of getting some flowers, but we just moved, you know," my mom responded.

"That's no excuse for ignoring the trends of the season sweetie. Look, perhaps after my soaps today I can give you some pointers. Oh! That reminds me, have you *seen* what was happening on Days of Our World yesterday? Imagine, a secret twin brother from Algeria!"

And then suddenly the conversation was about soap operas. My mom was so engrossed in the conversation that I was able to sneak out of the room without either of them noticing.

Basset and I went over to Genevieve's to hear more news from around the neighborhood. There was a new rabbit at the O'Hanley's that was making the dog that already lived there really jealous, and there were rumors of a budding romance between two collies up the street.

Basset wasn't a fan of Genevieve's "news." He called her a gossip when we weren't around her, and told me not to spend too much time "filling my head with that junk."

He was always civil and polite to her, and though he tried to keep me from spending too much time with her, it was Basset that first introduced me to Genevieve.

When I asked him why he still spent time with her if he didn't like the gossip, he just said he thought Genevieve had a good heart.

Anyway, Basset kept introducing me around town, and I got to meet a family of hedgehogs and a bunch of dogs, a few cats, and Basset warned me about which dogs to steer clear of and which cats were particularly uppity. Genevieve even introduced me to a couple squirrels. They seemed to be nice enough – a little rude sometimes and pretty annoying with their high-pitched voices and nonstop talking – but not too bad.

"So are there any animals that can't talk?" I asked Basset one afternoon.

"Well of course," he said, like it was the most obvious thing in the world. "Mostly little things. Insects don't talk for instance, which is good. I don't think they'd have much to talk about, and it makes me feel better about eating the occasional bug, knowing they can't talk. Although I suppose they could talk, and I just can't understand them. Like how you couldn't understand me. Best not to think about it."

"What about mice?"

"Ah, that's a touchy subject. Most mice can't, but every once in a while you find one who can say a word or two. Cats promise they don't eat any mice who can talk, but some of us dogs think they shouldn't risk eating *any*. It's a bit of a debate."

It was one of the best weeks of my life, even with Mrs. Maplewood's visits. I still felt lonely sometimes without a friend to share it all with, but I was exploring a whole new world, and was making a lot of new non-human friends, which was nice.

And, of course, that's when things started to go bad.

Chapter 6

THE DISAPPEARANCE

It started off more weird than bad, but we could tell something big was coming, right from the start. Something big and mean.

It started with the disappearance of the birds.

I woke up exactly one week after Basset started talking and saw him sitting at the window, staring into the backyard with a sad look on his face.

I'd never seen him do that before. When he looked outside he always looked excited, like he couldn't wait to get out there and start chasing squirrels around for some revenge.

"What's wrong boy?" I asked, quickly getting up.

"I don't know," he said slowly. "But something's definitely wrong. I can't put my paw on it, but it's out there."

I sat next to him, wrapping my arm around his neck.

"I don't see anything," I said.

"Neither do I. I don't smell anything either…"

Suddenly I felt it too, a chill rising from the wood floor into my feet, up my ankles and tingling its way into my stomach. I knew something was wrong with this morning, something that made it feel cold.

"The birds!" I shouted all of a sudden, jumping back up to

my feet. "I don't hear any birds!"

That's why the morning felt so cold. The only time we didn't hear birds first thing in the morning was when they had all flown south for the winter.

Basset didn't move, but that sad look grew even deeper.

"Where did they go?"

"Do you think they finally got tired of the cats chasing them around and moved somewhere else?" I asked. I knew that made no sense, but I couldn't think of anything that did.

Basset shook his head.

"Cats and birds don't get along, but it's never broken out into war. Besides, there are cats everywhere around the world. Where could they move?"

I knew he was right.

I rushed downstairs to tell my parents about it, but they didn't think it was weird at all. They just didn't have time to really think about it.

"Our yard must have run out of worms or something," my dad said, not even looking up from his morning paper, which had the headline "Masked Marauder strikes silence: radio store cleared out."

I had seen word of the Masked Marauder in the news a few times recently, or overheard the name as I walked to school, but I hadn't really paid much attention. Some kind of criminal, a burglar or something.

I try not to pay too close attention to the news.

It focuses too much on getting people's attention, which usually means scaring people or shocking them.

Or lying to them. That works too.

Also, I'm a kid. Better things to do than sit and watch local news anchors try to drum up viewers and not trip over the teleprompter.

But I made a quick note to myself to read that paper when my dad was done with it. I had a hazy memory of a nightmare I'd had a few nights ago, maybe something about someone in a mask.

It had me intrigued.

My mom was busy scraping the burnt part off a piece of toast.

"You worry too much," she said. "What disaster could possibly have caused the birds to leave? This isn't one of your fantasy stories."

If only she knew how wrong she was.

At that moment Basset padded silently into the room.

"Adults won't notice it," he said sadly. "At least not for a while. They're too busy to notice little things like that, too much else going on in their minds and in front of their eyes. Besides, they wouldn't *want* to see something different about their lives. That makes things too complicated."

I knew he was right. How many times had my mom gotten a new haircut that my dad didn't notice? Or how many times had my dad washed and buffed the car and gotten frustrated when mom didn't comment on how awesome it looked?

Or how often did I get a good grade, stick it on the fridge, and take it down a few weeks later without anyone saying anything?

A lot. That's how often.

It never really upset me before. People are busy and distracted. But with something this serious it definitely mattered.

And Basset and I were alone.

"I'm heading out to take a look around," I said. Neither of my parents looked up as I raced out the back door.

Basset and I went straight to the woods. On most mornings at this time there would be dozens of birds pecking away at the ground while it was still soft from the dew. This morning it was completely deserted.

Once we got under the cover of the trees we both looked up at the branches. Usually you'd hear a few sparrows or mourning doves up there, but all we heard today was the creaking of the empty branches.

"What's going on?" I whispered.

"I don't know. But I don't like it," he whispered back. "Humans might not know it, but the animal world usually makes a lot of sense. Birds don't just pack up and go on vacation."

He put his nose to the wet ground and started sniffing around.

"There's still plenty of worms too," he said.

"Oh come on. Are you telling me you can smell worms underground?" I asked skeptically.

Basset glanced up at me, his nose slightly upturned, looking extremely proud of himself. "Of course I can. This nose doesn't miss a thing."

He kept sniffing around the trees and through the undergrowth, pausing every once in a while to show off.

"Squirrel was here yesterday, headed up the oak tree and is still sleeping in there…"

"Rabbit and family were over here Tuesday…."

"Oh boy, smells like one of the raccoons found a big load of trash last night and dragged it through here…"

Finally he stopped and stiffened.

"What is it boy?"

"Nothing, I…I just thought I heard something. Something too high pitched for human ears to hear but… it must have been nothing. It's gone now."

His head was still cocked to the side.

"No sign of the birds though?" I asked

"Oh, there's sign," he said. "They were here last night, all of them. I can smell them all over the place. But they all left. At the exact same time, too."

Suddenly I heard a twig snap behind me.

I whirled around and at the same instant Basset ran off in another direction, like he had picked up the scent of a squirrel.

I peered as hard as I could into the gloom, but at first I saw nothing. I knew I had heard something, and it sounded like something large, but my sweeping eyes didn't see anything.

Then I saw them.

Eyes.

Chapter 7

THE EYES IN THE FOREST

Two curious eyes were looking right at me out of the darkness a good distance away.

I stumbled back a couple steps in my surprise, but the eyes didn't move. Whatever it was was just curious.

My vision started to adjust a bit as I snuck closer, and that's when I realized what, and who, it was.

Standing in the darkness, just looking at me, was a girl I had seen a couple of times in school, though I didn't know her name. I'd never talked to her. In fact, I didn't think I'd even heard her talk, not even once.

I could be forgiven for not noticing her at first in the forest. You don't normally expect to see a girl as tall as a tree in the woods.

The girl was tall, and I mean massively tall. I knew she was about my age as I'd seen her walking around school sometimes, but she was definitely over six feet tall. That's tall for a boy, but for a girl it's practically unheard of. She had a kind face that I always thought was pretty, from what I could see from all the way down here, of course. She had extremely wide shoulders that she carried high, like she was always preparing to defend herself.

Her hair was shaggy but not very long, just kind of messy

and cut unevenly, so in the darkness it looked almost like leaves fluttering in the breeze.

She kept looking at me like she couldn't decide whether she should turn and leave or not, like she couldn't decide if she liked me. Then Basset walked from around one of the trees behind me and came up to my side.

As soon as the girl saw him, she motioned for me to come over.

Now, I don't usually approach tree-sized kids in abandoned woods. That's a good way to lose your lunch money. Or a couple of teeth. Or both. Girls can be bullies too, you know, and while boys don't usually admit to being scared of a girl, when they're six feet tall you have to at least admit to being . . . cautious.

But for some reason I felt like I could trust her. I don't know why, but maybe it was the fact that Basset immediately started to trot up to her. If Basset trusted her, so would I.

The closer I got, the more it seemed the girl wanted to turn and run. I didn't get it. She was big enough to squash Basset and I with one swing of her hand, like two extremely unlucky spiders.

But her face looked tortured, like she wanted more than anything to run away or disappear, and for some reason she was convincing herself to stand still.

I knew the feeling. I got it often enough in school.

When I was a few feet away, the girl stammered out "Uh...um...hi..."

I stopped.

"Hi," I responded. "My name's Nate." It was a weird place for an introduction, but I still had my manners, even in a forest.

"I know," she responded, looking down at her feet for a second before looking back at my eyes. "I mean, I see you around school. What are you doing out in the woods?"

Before I could respond, she blurted out "Oh! I'm Sam by

the way."

I guess she remembered her manners too.

I didn't really want to tell her what I was doing in the woods (talking dog, disappearing birds, all that), but I didn't want to lie either. Not the best way to start off with a new person.

"You know my name, but you've never introduced yourself before? Why here in the woods?"

She looked at her feet again, her ratty size 11 boots shuffling in the leaves and making as much racket as a dancing Clydesdale (which is a thing, but that's another story).

"I don't talk much, I guess."

"Me neither. I mean, I do, just not at school."

We had an awkward silence for a couple of seconds. I wanted to find out more about her – where she lived, what she liked to do in this town, why such a tall girl would be so shy and quiet – but I wasn't sure how to do that. It had been too long since I'd made new friends.

"So what were you doing in the woods?" she asked again. "It's not that I mind, I'm just curious, you know."

"Just exploring. What were you doing back here?"

She shrugged. "Same thing I guess." Then she sighed, looking up at the trees. "Wondering where the birds got off to."

"You noticed that too!" I said, before I could stop myself.

She didn't seem to think it was strange at all.

"Of course I did. Who wouldn't notice when all the birds suddenly disappear?"

"Most people, actually. My parents didn't. Most people wouldn't notice if the birds all changed color and were suddenly hot pink."

She nodded. "Most people don't look around themselves, I guess. Sleepwalking through life. I came back here to see if I could figure out what happened, where the birds went."

"Me too," I said.

She glanced down at Basset again.

"You can pet him and say hi if you want," I said. "I know he'd like that. He loves new people."

Basset turned and smiled at me.

"Sure do," he whispered.

Sam hesitated. "I…I'd better not."

"Why not? He won't bite."

"It's not that…It's just…I don't have a dog. My parents won't let me, and I don't know what to do."

"Well it's real easy. Just stroke his fur back, and maybe give him a little scratch behind the ears."

Sam slowly put out a hand the size of a frying pan, and gently rubbed Basset's head. I've never seen anyone be that gentle with anything. It was like she was handling a million dollar comic book, and was afraid she'd rip the pages.

The more time she spent petting Basset, the easier it seemed to get for her, until she was smiling a little.

"Why won't your parents let you have a dog?" I asked while she started to scratch Basset behind the ears.

She hesitated. "They just…they won't, that's all."

I knew not to push it.

"Sorry."

"It's okay."

She looked up from Basset after a few more seconds. "Look, I'm sorry I never introduced myself to you before. I know you're new and noticed no one seemed to talk to you but…I figured you wouldn't want to talk to me."

I was surprised.

"Why wouldn't I want to talk to you?"

"Well no one else does. I'm tall."

"I noticed," I laughed. Sam blushed a bright crimson. "I'm

sorry. It's just…why would that make me not want to talk to you?"

"I'm big and I'm clumsy. People are either afraid of me, or they tease me because I'm always knocking into stuff. I can't even fit in my desk and have to sit on the floor in the back. Besides, everyone thinks it's weird for a girl to be this tall."

I smiled. "Kids don't want to talk to me because I'm small. I always wished I was bigger. Guess kids will be mean either way."

"I'm sorry," she said.

"It's not your fault."

"Yeah, but sometimes I feel like it is. Because I'm so big, no one can push me around. But you… well I've seen what Guster Liberman and his guys do to you."

I shrugged. "Still not your fault. But if you wanted to stop it, why didn't you?"

"I don't want to hurt anyone," she said.

"It's okay. Really. Those kids are just jerks."

"Yeah," she smiled. "Jerks."

At that moment Basset pricked his ears up again and cocked his head to the side.

"What is it boy?" I asked. "Is it that sound again?"

When I turned to look at Sam, she had the oddest look on her face. It was like she was studying me.

I slipped up. I knew I shouldn't have talked to Basset like he could talk back. But there was no way Sam could have figured out that Basset could talk to me; not from such a small comment. It was a weird thing to say, sure, but I shouldn't worry about it. That would just be paranoid. Who would jump to the conclusion that my dog talks to me?

Sam sighed.

"Look, I notice things, okay? Don't freak out, but I'm pretty good at picking up on stuff, even subtle, little stuff. It's gotten me in more trouble than I like to think about so I usually

41

keep my mouth shut but... can your dog talk to you?"

Chapter 8

THE FORT

My mouth hung open and I just stared at her.

"Yeah, I thought so," she continued. "See, this is a good example. Most people see you with your mouth hanging open and think 'he thinks I'm crazy for asking that question. He's shocked by my stupidity.' But no. You're shocked because I *know*."

I snapped my mouth closed, but still didn't know what to say.

"It's okay, really. I won't tell anyone. Promise."

I swallowed hard.

"If I told anyone I thought my dog was talking to me, they'd think I was crazy, or a really bad liar. But you believe he can talk to me without any convincing?"

She shrugged. "There's a lot in this world we don't know about. Who am I to say talking animals can't happen?"

"That's the first conclusion you jump to though?"

"Not usually. This is the first time anything weird like this has happened in my life too. I don't believe in aliens or ghosts or anything like that. I've never jumped to a conclusion like this in my life. But don't you see? I saw it in your face."

"But I could be lying to you."

"With your face? I don't think so. Besides why would you? You *want* people to think you're crazy or something?"

"Good point."

"That would be a stupid lie. So if you aren't lying and you aren't crazy, it has to be true." She shrugged her wide shoulders again. Must be a favorite mannerism. "So I guess it's true."

She was taking this a bit easier than I did at first, that's for sure. And I had the benefit of actually *hearing* the animals.

"Look, you seem nicer than most kids in school," she continued. "You haven't teased me about my size, and you haven't even mentioned my lisp," to be honest, I hadn't even noticed it, it was so slight it was hardly noticeable, but to Sam I'm sure it was all she heard when she talked "and I'm really curious about this talking dog thing. Do you think…." And then she trailed off.

It was like she couldn't force the words out of her mouth, like they were stuck in her head. I understood completely. Sometimes you're too scared of being disappointed, so scared you don't even risk trying. But all you get by not trying is *guaranteed* disappointment.

"Sure, we can hang out," I said, like she had asked.

She was trying not to show it, but she was clearly excited. She didn't want to seem desperate, I guess, and kids our age don't want to look vulnerable by getting too excited or emotional, but you could tell. Her eyes were smiling.

Besides, I felt the same way. I hadn't talked to a kid my own age outside of school since my first day here in town. They talked to me, but teasing doesn't really count as conversation, does it?

"We can't go to my place," I continued. "My parents don't know you, and they're already at work. They won't like me bringing a stranger over."

She nodded, not even asking why I didn't just lie to my

parents. "Look, my old man would kill me if I brought a friend over, but I've got a little fort back in the woods. Want to check it out?"

I nodded.

I followed Sam deeper into the woods, not following any path that I could see, but she clearly knew where she was going. She lumbered along like a giant, stomping through the leaves and smaller shrubs, but she was fast. She didn't stop or pause to look for landmarks like familiar stones or bent trees. It was like she'd lived out here her whole life.

"You live around here?" I asked as we walked.

"Yeah. In a tiny house on Maple Avenue," she jerked her head in the direction we had come from. "Been there ever since I was born. It's cramped, even though it's just me and Dad most of the time, so I spend a lot of time out here. Even in winter."

I smiled. It was nice to finally meet someone else in this town who liked the outdoors as much as I did, even though it seemed she spent most of her time out here because she *had* to.

Most kids were too busy on video games.

"I like it out here," she continued. "It's quiet. Nothing bad happens out in the woods, no other people to deal with. Just the animals, and most of them are friendly enough." She gave a tiny, almost imperceptible smile to Basset.

I turned and looked at my dog, giving him a look that said "She seem alright to you, boy?"

"She's a nice kid," Basset whispered. "I've seen her around the neighborhood before. She feeds birds and sometimes even the squirrels. She could pick her friends better, but it's nice just the same."

I chuckled to myself. Basset just couldn't get over anyone liking squirrels.

"Did he say something?" Sam asked, kind of worried, like

she'd had people talking behind her back more than enough. "What'd he say?"

"He likes you."

Sam didn't say anything, but her eyes were smiling again.

Before long we came to a thick hedge, probably eight feet tall, that went deep into the woods on both sides. The hedge was covered in thorns long enough to break through the skin and cause some serious bleeding. There was no way around.

Sam just kept walking.

She disappeared into the hedge (with way less rustling than I had expected, and no bloodcurdling scream either), and a second later her head popped out.

It looked intact.

"I scraped all the thorns off and left only the smaller branches in this spot," for the first time she really smiled, and she looked as proud as I did when I'd shown off some of Basset's tricks to my friends back home.

My old home, I mean.

"You can walk right through without getting hurt, and the branches just slap back into place. Perfect hiding spot."

I didn't ask what she was hiding from. Sometimes we all need someplace.

Someplace that's just ours.

I stepped forward, still a little nervous that I'd get pricked by a hundred wooden needles, but I came out the other side without a scratch or mark on me.

Just a few leaves in my hair.

Basset followed, his tongue hanging out and his tail wagging to be exploring a new spot.

I was surprised he didn't immediately start sniffing around, but I think he was too curious to hear more about Sam.

Sniffing could wait.

I looked up from my dog, and my jaw dropped.

Again.

Sam had called this a "little fort."

Sure. Little. The same way Sam was short. The same way an elephant would be "a cute pet."

The hedge went all the way around a small clearing, about three times the size of my bedroom, and most of the space was taken up by a building.

Not a fort. I said a building, and that's what it was.

Sam had constructed it out of plywood and old boards, either tied together with string or hammered with rusty nails, but she had done some amazing work. The roof was seven feet off the ground, and the walls looked sturdy enough to hold up for years, even through the nastiest storms. It had a few windows covered in wax paper to let light in, and even had a massive oak front door with three bolt locks on it.

"You like it?" Sam asked, looking at her feet again nervously.

"It's amazing! How did you do it?"

Sam looked a little embarrassed at my praise, but she was clearly proud too.

"It took a long time, but I know a thing or two about building stuff. My dad works construction when he can find the jobs, and he showed me a bit when I was little. The rest I picked up just by trying. I'll show you around."

The fort had clearly been built in sections. The first part, with the door, looked like the oldest: the walls were a little crooked and sagged here and there, but the further back you went down the long, skinny building the better it got.

"I found this old door back in the woods a few years ago, just tossed out here by someone who was done with it, and that's what gave me the idea to build this place."

47

She gestured at the building like it was the easiest thing in the world.

She approached the door, and to my surprise she didn't reach for the latch.

She reached to the other side of the door, and flipped the hinges up. Hidden underneath the hinges were three bolt locks. She slid those to the side, and the door opened.

"There's hinges on the inside," she said. "You can't see them from out here. It's a little security system I came up with." She looked embarrassed again. "It's kinda silly, I know. There's nothing in here to steal. But it makes me feel safer."

"It's brilliant!" I said, without even thinking. Her blush deepened. "But it is! No one could get in, and I'd never have thought of it."

She led me in through the door, into a large room with lots of used furniture that Sam had clearly fixed up.

There was a dining room table with a broken leg repaired with an old railroad tie, a few chairs with rusty stop signs for seats, a potbelly wood stove, and – my favorite – a rowboat she had turned into a bookcase.

It was loaded with some of my favorite books, but they were all tattered paperbacks or moldy copies that the library had thrown away.

"You like to read?" I asked.

"Sure, of course," she shrugged again. "Takes my mind off things, I guess."

I went over for a closer look. I know I should have been inspecting her impressive "fort," but my first instinct was to take a look at her books.

There were all the classics, from C.S. Lewis to Tolkien to Douglas Adams, and six of the Harry Potter books. She even had Dean Koontz.

"I'm surprised," I said.

"Oh," she looked devastated, absolutely devastated. I didn't mean anything by it, but she looked like I'd told her that her favorite sports player was injured and would never play again.

"I get it," she said. "People don't think I'm smart. It's because I'm so big, and because I talk kinda slow, and because of my lisp. Teachers don't even call on me because they don't want to offend 'the slow kid.' But I'm not slow. Not in my head. I just talk slow."

"Ohmygosh!" I blurted out in one big word. "I didn't mean that! I just meant I was surprised that you liked all the same books I do! I didn't think I'd find another kid here who liked Koontz. I mean, it's not exactly kid-friendly stuff, so most parents don't let their kids read it."

She looked at me warily, like she was trying to decide if a strange dog on the street was friendly or a rabid beast.

"I'm serious! I'll even let you borrow the last Harry Potter book if you want."

She made up her mind.

"Really?!" she beamed at me. "I thought I'd have to wait until the library copy got worn out."

I wanted to know why she couldn't get her own copy (paperback was like five bucks), but didn't want to be rude.

I smiled back.

"Seriously. It's so cool you like that stuff too."

I wanted to chat with her about all my favorite books, see what she thought of the latest Odd Thomas story or what she thought of the Lord of the Rings movies versus the books, but that wasn't the first thing we had to discuss. After taking a tour, she'd want to know more about Basset.

Sam showed me around her creation, which had three separate rooms, and a winding metal staircase leading up onto the roof.

"I found that thing in a scrap pile. It took a lot of fixing up, but it's sturdy. Has to be," she said with a laugh, indicating her height.

She was getting a little more comfortable with me.

Basset stayed at my heels for a while, interested in our conversation, but he couldn't help himself for long. He quickly went off and started sniffing all the corners.

I'd have to remember to ask him later why he *had* to go sniffing things. It was almost obsessive compulsive.

There was more recycled furniture, but everything was surprisingly clean and sturdy.

When we were done, Sam led us back to the dining room table and folded herself down on a chair topped with an old couch cushion that looked like it had the exact same pattern as my grandmother's sofa.

"I usually like to sit up on the roof, but it's windy today," she said. "And I want to be able to hear everything. If you'll tell me, of course."

I did.

Chapter 9
THE INVESTIGATION BEGINS

I had wanted to tell someone about the talking animals from the first moment it started, and now that I finally had the chance the words all came spilling out of me like word diarrhea.

Gross analogy. But it fits.

I told her everything: about how Basset first talked to me, about meeting the other animals in town, and about noticing the birds disappearing that morning. She didn't interrupt at all, but sat with an interested look on her face. I was sure she'd have questions, but she was saving them until I was done.

"I thought I was crazy, and maybe I am, but I don't think so," I said at the end. "I don't know why, but as insane as this is, I just feel like it's real. But that's probably what a crazy person would say."

"Crazy people usually don't think they're crazy," Sam said. "I always thought there was more to life than the humdrum mundane crap adults think there is. Go to school, get a job, die. There's more than that, right? Well this just proves it."

I nodded. "I've always felt the same way."

She sat for a minute, thinking to herself.

"So what does Basset think happened to the birds?"

I turned to look at my dog, who was sniffing under a fancy

side table.

When he noticed me looking, he turned around with dust covering his nose and hanging down like a Santa Claus beard.

He returned with his face pointed down sheepishly.

"It's okay buddy, I know you can't help it."

"I'm just so curious! There's so much to smell!"

"I know. Look, Sam was wondering if you have any clue what happened to all the birds. I know earlier you had no idea, but have you thought of anything?"

He paused a moment, cocking his head curiously to the side.

"Nothing. Imagine one day all the police in town disappeared, or all the mailmen just vanished. That's how weird this is for me. I've got no explanation."

I turned to Sam, who was watching us with interest.

"I must look pretty crazy carrying on a conversation with a dog when you can't hear him talking back, huh?"

"You sure do," Sam laughed.

"Anyway, he said he has no idea. They just packed up and left, all at once."

"That's not good," Sam said, looking out one of the windows. "I don't know why, but I feel like there's something more going on here."

"I know what you mean. It feels so....wrong."

"It's bad," Basset said with that sad faraway look in his eyes. "It's worse than a trip to the vet. Something is happening here, and this is just the start."

I sat thinking for a minute, then remembered that Sam couldn't hear Basset, and snapped my head up.

"He says it's bad, by the way."

"I figured. You looked glum."

As I tell this story, I won't always tell you when I repeated conversations from animals for Sam. That would get tedious. So in general, it's probably safe to assume from here on out that I'm translating for Sam. Unless there was no time, of course.

We sat thinking for a little while. This fort was the perfect base of operations for exploring the woods or playing games of soldiers or cowboys or whatever, and it was a perfect spot for card games or reading, but I wasn't excited at all. I just couldn't stop wondering what had happened to the birds.

"Look, this is the first really weird thing that I've seen in my whole life," Sam said. "But it happened right after you first learned you could hear animals talk. Too much of a coincidence."

I nodded.

I had been thinking the same thing.

I didn't know what that meant, but it wasn't good.

"I think if anyone can figure this out, it's you. And Basset of course."

"What do you mean? I'm just a boy and his dog."

"The cops won't listen. Any adult out there will think we're crazy if we tell them the birds disappeared and it's a bad omen. But you, you *know* the animals, you can find out what's going on. You *have* to solve this. It's up to you."

I shuddered. That's a lot of pressure.

"You want to help?" I asked, suddenly excited. If I had a friend with me this would be a whole lot easier. It could even turn out to be fun.

"What can I do?"

"You can help me figure this out. You might not be able to talk to animals, but you're smart. You can help solve this."

"I'd love to help if I can," Sam looked embarrassed. "Not sure how much help I'll be, but I'll do what I can."

"Perfect," I heard Basset say beside me. "Maybe we can figure this out."

"Chances are we're getting worked up for nothing," I said. "Overactive imaginations. When I was ten I saw some strangers in black cloaks hanging around town, and was convinced they were a gang of bank robbers. I looked like an idiot when I warned my parents about it and they told me the men were just monks visiting the local church. It'll be embarrassing if it turns out the birds just got scared off by a new cat or something. We'd look like a toddler getting scared of a plastic spider."

"I don't think we're just imagining this," Sam responded. "There's no simple explanation."

"So what should we do?"

"You and Basset go around and talk to the other animals. See if anyone saw anything or heard anything unusual. My guess is the animals are paying closer attention to all this than humans are."

"Some," Basset said.

I nodded.

"We'll head out then. Boy, I wish I could hang out here some more," I said in an off-hand way, barely noticing I said it.

Sam had a huge smile.

"Maybe once this is all settled?" she said, like she was almost afraid of the answer.

"Definitely. Listen, Sam, why don't you come with us while I talk to the animals?"

"You don't think the animals will mind? I mean, I don't know them."

"I think it'll be fine. Most of them are trusting, and the more cautious ones know Basset."

"Most of us are good judges of character too," Basset said.

When I told Sam that, she smiled shyly.

We headed out of the fort and back into the forest, which was eerily quiet.

"Where should we start?" I asked.

"We should talk to the animals who live near the edge of the forest," Basset said.

At the exact same time Sam said "Probably with the animals near the woods," which made me laugh.

We started off three houses south of my house, at the corner of Maple and Elm streets, which were the border to the woods.

Neither the Pomeranian nor the black cat had seen anything.

Same story two houses down, where a collie named Paulie had slept through the whole morning.

The cats next door were wondering what happened to the birds, but had no more ideas than we did.

"There has got to be a faster way," Sam said. "Hey, I don't know how it works in the animal world, but anytime my mom wants to know something, she calls up Mrs. Maplewood. She blathers on about all the latest gossip and knows what *everyone* has been up to. No point in talking to anyone else."

"Of course!" I shouted. "Genevieve!"

Chapter 10

GENEVIEVE

Basset looked up at me in surprise, then looked down embarrassed, like when my parents came in after he had been rummaging through the trash.

"I should've thought of that. Sorry buddy."

"It's okay," I said, explaining to Sam.

Sam got down on her knees and scratched behind Basset's ears.

"You can't think of everything," she said in a surprisingly small, soothing voice. "Don't put too much on your shoulders."

Basset looked up into Sam's eyes, and licked her hand.

"He says thank you," I told her.

"So who's Genevieve?" Sam asked as we made our way down to her house. "I mean, I'm assuming she's the town animal-gossip, but who is she?"

"She's a cat," I started.

"Ah, of course."

I smirked. "A massive Persian about the size and shape of a bowling ball. She's sweet, but you have to take everything she says with a grain of salt. She's more interested in telling a good story than telling the truth."

"Same as Mrs. Maplewood."

As we continued walking down the street, we were greeted by Mr. Barston, the county librarian, on his way to work.

"Good morning children," he said, tipping his cap in our direction.

We nodded back.

Ken Barston is one of the few friendly people I'd met in town. I'd go into the library often to check out new books, and he would always chat with me about what he was reading.

He looked like a librarian, too. Large round glasses with thick metal rims, spidery white hair that stuck up all over the place, rather tall and lanky, with his eyes always looking kind of dazed and dreamy. I liked him.

Before long we arrived at Genevieve's house. I'm sure her owners would have preferred we call it "The Johnsons' house," but obviously that wasn't true. It was Genevieve's.

We walked right up the front lawn, through a rusty iron gate, and into the enclosed backyard.

The Johnsons never minded me coming by. Most people in the neighborhood let me wander around, actually. The adults were a close-knit group, and it was a sleepy little village, so the kids could mostly come and go wherever they pleased.

When we came into the backyard, I don't think Sam saw Genevieve at first. But when she did, her eyes grew wide and round as saucers.

That's how I was when I first saw her.

Genevieve spent most of the day sunning herself on a large gray boulder, and when she curled up and slept she looked exactly like she was a part of the rock. Same color gray, her flat face smooth as a stone, and her massive rolly-polly body made her look like a boulder alright.

But once she moved, even the slightest bit, you knew there was nothing solid about her.

This cat jiggled.

"Ahhh, good morning Basset," she purred, stretching herself out like a sausage being pulled on both ends. "Was hoping you'd stop by. Heard some just delicious news about Frankie and Delilah, the two poodles on the next block."

Basset gave her a disapproving look. He didn't much like gossip.

"It's a secret of course," she said "and I shouldn't tell, but I know you'd get it out of me sooner or later so I might as well just give it to you without a struggle."

I could tell he wanted to bare his teeth, but he was holding back. We needed her to be talkative today.

"We came to ask you if know anyone who saw anything unusual today or last night," Basset said.

Genevieve perked right up. She sat up straight, making her rolls of flesh ripple and bend like Jell-o sitting on a washing machine.

"Ooooh, someone's a curious boy," Genevieve purred. "What's with the questions? You're usually so disinterested in my stories."

"Well today I'm asking. Has anyone seen anything unusual?"

"Oh of course someone has," she said. "But who, I wonder? What's this all about?"

"I'm assuming you've noticed the birds have gone missing?" I asked.

"I wondered what happened to them myself," she said, clearly surprised by the news but unwilling to admit it. "I like to give them a little chase in the morning, like any good cat."

The only animal Genevieve could ever catch would be a slug. And that would be an exhausting, day-long hunt.

But you don't insult a cat's pride. Especially if that cat

happens to be a 50 pound gossiping Persian named Genevieve.

I knew how to deal with people like Genevieve. Or animals, I mean. It's the same thing. Flattery. That's what gossips are after.

"We knew no one else could help us," I said. "You know more about this neighborhood than anyone else."

She purred deeply and closed her eyes.

"Of course I do. But before I help you out, perhaps you can help me?"

Basset was trying to keep calm, but there was a slight growl in his throat.

"What do you want?"

"Oh, nothing much. Just a secret or two. You're always so quiet, Bassy. So private."

"He has a right to be," I said back. It was reflex. I would stand up for Basset no matter what.

Basset gave me a proud look that said "thank you."

I was glad I'd stuck up for him, but I knew Genevieve didn't respond well to force. She'd just curl back up in a furry ball and ignore us if we didn't play along.

"Someone's in a bad mood today," she said, looking from me to Basset. "You really should keep a better leash on your human."

Basset gave me one of his looks that said "sorry," but he was smart enough not to respond or snap at the cat.

"I've already given you enough juicy news for free today," she purred out. "What have you got for me? I know you've heard things even I haven't," she said to me. "You're ears are so much further off the ground. You can hear all sorts of good things."

"I tell you some gossip, you tell me yours in return?" I asked.

"Oh, no no no!" she hissed. "I do *not* gossip. I merely

spread the news. The animals have a right to know. It's a useful, noble profession, you know."

"Sorry, Genny, that's not what I meant. Of course. News for news. Now let's see, what's particularly juicy? Something about Franklin, the puggle next door? Or Angelise, the black cat across the street? I saw some particularly odd behavior from her the other day."

I knew teasing her was the best way to draw her out. Genevieve sat up straight, like she spotted a treat in my hand.

"Oh? Odd behavior? But Angelise has always been so prim and proper. What's she been up to?"

She sounded practically starving.

Before I could continue, Sam laughed behind me.

"Oooh, or perhaps we could tell you about the cat who's been stealing cream from her owners after the milkman drops it off?" she said. "That's a nasty one for sure."

Genevieve got that shocked look cats get when you start up the vacuum, when they freeze for a second before bolting for cover.

"What? What's that? I mean, who? How…"

"You're such a well-groomed cat, Genny," she said. "But you're not very good at wiping off your mouth."

She hastily licked her paws and cleaned off her face before she even had a chance to think about it.

"Sorry for interrupting," Sam said. "Go ahead."

"Thanks," I whispered. "I was bluffing. Good one."

"Any time."

"So, Genny. You want me to spread the news on that one, right? The public has a right to know, after all."

She blinked. I think she wanted to run away, but all the cream had gone straight to her hips. And her sides. Basically all of her, to be honest. She couldn't run. She was more a waddler, and occasionally a trip-and-roll-er.

"Or, you could just tell us what you know," I continued. "You have a noble profession, after all."

I could hear Sam holding back a laugh behind me, with a snort or two.

Genevieve shot her an icy look. Her pride had taken enough of a beating for the day.

"Of course," she lifted her nose high. "I was going to tell you. After all, I don't need any humans to be informants for me. I'm good enough at what I do without your help. I was just teasing, that's all sweetie. A little feline repartee, you know."

"Of course. Repartee. I knew it all along." My sarcasm was thicker than cream, but cats don't get sarcasm. They're known for their lack of a sense of humor, actually.

You probably suspected that.

"Let's see…ah yes," she returned to her curled up position. "Franklin saw that little weasel running from the woods early this morning. You know something's up when he runs out in daylight and in the open. He loves the shadows, that one. But there he was, as bold as you like, as bold as a dog begging at the table. You want to know what happened in the woods last night, ask the weasel."

"Thank you Genevieve. Good news, as always."

"Any time dear. That's what I'm here for. Now, if you don't mind, I think I could use a nap. It's been a long day."

It was only 11 a.m., but I didn't argue.

We left the way we came, and headed back for the woods, while I relayed to Sam what Genevieve had said about the weasel.

"A weasel, huh? I've never been that close to one. Are they dangerous?"

I looked at Basset for the answer. I'd never met the neighborhood weasel. Basset had always said I wasn't ready to.

"Oh yes. Definitely," Basset answered. "Always be careful

around a weasel."

Dealing with a weasel can be tricky. And "dangerous" is just the beginning.

Chapter 11
THE WEASEL'S GAME

"What's the weasel's name?" Sam asked.

"That's the thing about weasels. No one knows his name. You'll see."

We reached the edge of the woods, and I let Basset lead the way. He quickly took us to the left, down a path that no human eyes could see, but that a dog's nose could follow without pausing.

"How did you do that earlier?" I asked Sam. "How did you know how to deal with Genevieve? You could only hear half the conversation. My half."

"I was able to figure it out," she said with one of her patented shrugs. "It was easy enough to spot the cream on her whiskers, and then I just had to mention it to her the right way. I was just following your lead."

"You're good at that," I said. "Figuring things out I mean."

"I guess."

As we walked I explained weasels to Sam.

My first day meeting all the village animals, Basset told me which animals to steer clear of, and the one he spent the most time on was the weasel.

He didn't tell me they were *particularly* dangerous, but he told me to steer clear just the same. They're more trouble than they're worth.

Weasels are pathological liars.

That's something most people don't know about weasels.

Also that they can talk. Most people don't know that either I suppose, making it hard for them to know weasels even *can* lie, but there you have it.

It's a game to them, Basset said. A weasel won't even talk to you if you aren't joining in the lying game. That's how you earn a weasel's respect: lie. A lot.

But you have to tell the truth at the same time, bury it deep so the weasel has to dig to find it.

The trick is to know what's a lie and what's the truth.

It's a dangerous game.

Before long we came to an old rotten stump, covered in moss and mushrooms. Underneath was a tiny hole: the weasel's den.

There was no way to tell if he was home or not, and I wasn't about to stick my head in the dark hole to find out.

We just had to hope he'd want to come out and play.

"Weasel? Weasel, are you home?" Basset asked. "It's me...um...Bass...et. Dang."

Basset's terrible at lying.

A long red snout poked its way out of the hole, followed by the rest of a pointed face and two shrewd eyes shining in the gloom.

"Poor show, Basset my boy," the weasel said, slinking the rest of the way out of the hole and perching himself at the entrance. "You never come to visit, and I can't even begin to imagine why."

Each animal has a distinct voice, even though their mouths don't move. The weasel's voice sounded like a cockney British accent, and he whispered like he was trying to get your attention in a back alley to sell you something shady.

Basset was embarrassed by his failure to start with a good lie, but he quickly raised his head and sat up straight.

"You know full well, 'my boy,'" he responded. "I don't have the time or the taste for your games."

"Oh, tut tut. No fun at all, is he children?" The weasel asked, turning to look at me. "Oh, if it isn't the boy who can hear! I've heard so much about you! Even came to visit yesterday and introduce myself, but you were out and about I suspect."

That was clearly a lie. The game had begun.

"Nice to meet you," I said. Good to start off with a lie right off the bat. "My name's Nate, and this is my friend Pennywhistle Thistlebranch."

The weasel looked impressed.

"Nice to meet ya' children. A right pleasure indeed. The name's Everglade Amsterdam," he swiftly bowed with a flourish of his front paw.

That was a lie, and Basset and I knew it.

Every single time he'd introduce himself the weasel would use a different name: Eustace Chiselbottom, Cherith Wonderstone, Hummingbird Saltalamacchia… he whipped them out so fast he must have made a list of hundreds of names and memorized it.

Or he was really good at lying.

Now, I said you can never *assume* anything about an animal just by his species, but it's usually a good idea to *suspect* something. Assuming and suspecting are different, and could be the difference between life and death.

For instance, you can't assume a lion will kill you. I mean, there are plenty of perfectly nice lions in the circus, and I've chatted with a few. But it's still best to be cautious around most of them. If I bumped into a lion on the street I wouldn't *assume* he was an evil child-eating monster, but I'd be plenty cautious.

65

You know, because he might eat me.

Thus the caution.

So I didn't want to be unfair and assume the weasel was a dangerous little critter, but I was cautious.

When he told us his name, Basset and I exchanged a look that said, "yeah right," but I wasn't about to accuse the weasel.

They hate being called liars.

Also, they have really sharp teeth.

It's best to be careful around a weasel. Unless you could use a few extra holes, that is.

Personally, I like my skin the way it is: holeless.

"A pleasure," I responded.

"So what brings ya children to me 'umble 'ome today? I have to tell ya though, I'm running a bit late for an engagement. Me and some chums are planning a good heist of some birds' nests later today. It always impresses the ladies."

Not sure how much of that was a lie, but it didn't really matter.

The social calendar of a weasel wasn't really what I came to find out.

"We're here on something similar, actually. I have a flock of birds by my house that I use to carry messages around town for me, but they seem to have up and vanished."

I was treading carefully now. I was going to say that I used the birds as transportation, that they picked me up and flew me to school in the morning, but that would have been ridiculous.

You have to tell *good* lies to a weasel.

That's important.

"And the sad thing is, I needed them to spy on some people over in the downtown," I continued. "I'm helping with a police investigation, you see."

It's also important to build yourself up. What's the point of a lie if it doesn't make you look better? That's what the weasels say at least.

A sharp weasel like this would be able to dig through my lies and straight to the core of my story as quickly as he could reach the yolk of an egg. He'd instantly figure out that I wanted to know about the birds disappearing.

Now I had to dig through *his* story.

"Of course, of course. The police dogs are always askin' fer me 'elp, but I'm far too busy, I tell 'em. They don't listen though. 'We need ya,' they'll say. 'Yer the best at sneakin' and skulkin' about.' Now I know that's the truth, but I just can't be bothered at the moment. Perhaps later."

"I definitely understand," I said, nodding solemnly. "I was originally too busy to help the police too." I was scrambling for a good reason that I was too busy, but the weasel was into his own story now.

"Why just last night, while I was doin' me skulkin', I noticed the oddest thing. Down by that big crashed spaceship I saw a turkey poacher. Almost wanted to stop 'im, but I was headin' to a raid on a black bear's den and didn't have the time to go on any adventures."

Spaceship? Whatever happened to realistic lies?

"Sorry kiddies, but I really must be runnin'," he said, and before I even had a chance to take a breath he slinked away into the shadows and was gone.

Well that was a bust.

"What in the world did that mean?" I asked Basset.

"Don't ask me. Talking to weasels always makes my head hurt."

"What'd he say?" Sam asked. "That conversation was a little harder to follow than the last one."

I laughed. It was hard for me too, and I had heard both

halves of it.

"You think he buried the truth in there somewhere?" Sam asked after I told her what the weasel said.

"I don't know."

Basset cocked his head to the side.

"The truth was in there. Weasels don't just tell lies. That's cheating. The game is only fun if you can find the truth. What's the fun of a puzzle if the pieces don't fit together in the end?"

I told this to Sam, and she nodded her head.

"So we have to throw out whatever's an obvious lie and see what's left," she said, sitting on a nearby rock. She was lost in thought for a few minutes.

"That doesn't leave us with a whole lot," I said. "Sounded like most of it was lies."

"We can get rid of anything he said about his afternoon plans, I think," Sam said. "The truth is probably about anything he said about last night, because that's what we asked him about."

"Feel free to toss out the black bear part, too," Basset huffed. "I wouldn't pick a fight with a bear, and that weasel's ten times smaller than I am."

"I'm twice as big as you, but I still wouldn't pick a fight with that weasel," I laughed.

Basset smiled at me. I guess he realized it was a silly thing to get offended about.

"But I agree. He's a tough guy, but he's not an idiot," I said.

"Okay, so that leaves us with the part about the spaceship and the turkey poacher," Sam said slowly.

"There are no turkey poachers around here," Basset said.

"I don't think that's even a thing," I responded.

"Well that part's obvious, right?" Sam asked.

We both stared at her.

"Ah. Guess not. Sorry." She looked embarrassed.

"It's okay, go ahead. I think you're sharper than I am, and I don't want to speak for Basset, but we both want to hear what you think."

"Sure do," Basset said, smiling and panting at Sam encouragingly.

"Well, alright," she was still nervous to share her theory, but she went ahead. "It's a lie, but there's truth in it, right? I think he was talking about birds in general when he said turkey. It's his way of telling us he's talking about the birds. And a poacher is someone who hunts or captures animals illegally. It's legal to *hunt* turkeys here though. So I was thinking, he must mean the person who captured or got rid of all the birds illegally."

"Of course!" I shouted.

"That's really smart," Basset said. "Tell her I said that, would you?"

I did, and Sam got up off the rock to pace some.

"So we know he saw the person who got rid of the birds," I said.

"And we know it was a person, not some freak weather or something," Sam added. "Definitely a person."

"But where?" I asked. "There's no such thing as a crashed spaceship. Do you think he was only willing to tell us that he saw something, not where he saw it?"

"Maybe," Sam said. "But I don't know. Would that be cheating?"

"Maybe not technically," Basset said. "But it would be a dirty trick. And that weasel has never seemed dirty to me."

"Okay then," I said. "We must have missed something in the other parts. The crashed spaceship must have been just a lie. No truth there."

Sam nodded, and kept pacing.

We went over everything else the weasel had said, word by word, until we were all exhausted and really, really tired of hearing those same cockney words over and over.

Finally Sam sat down in defeat, and banged her head on the back of the rock.

"Ow!" she said, and then quickly leapt up. "Hey!"

For a second I thought she'd been stung by something, but then I saw her face.

She was beaming.

"You said weasels always try to make their lies realistic, or close to the truth, right?"

"Yeah," I said slowly, trying to see where she was going with this. "But that part about the spaceship's not realistic at all."

"Exactly! Don't you see? That means he was trying to draw our attention to it. So we wouldn't miss it. He's saying that's the most important part of his lie."

I felt slow, but it was starting to make sense to me.

The weasel was taking it easy on me, either because I was a first timer or because everyone in the village respected Basset so much. But he was telling me which part of his lie was the most important.

"So what does it mean then?"

"I'm working it out," she said.

"Crashed spaceship. Crashed spaceship. Crashed. Space. Ship."

She smacked her palm against her forehead.

"Of course!" Sam said. "Sheesh, he's good at this."

I laughed.

"He sure is. But I'm not. Care to let me in?" I smiled.

"Crashed. That's easy, it's not even a lie at all. Space, as in empty. And ship, as in shipment. The old empty train compartment crashed back in the woods."

The abandoned train compartment I'd visited a few times deeper in the forest. Of course. Now that she said it, it seemed so obvious.

I felt kind of embarrassed, but mostly I was excited. We were actually on the trail now.

And I had a friend to share it with.

Chapter 12
THE "CRASHED SPACESHIP"

We started running into the woods, excited to see the next part of this mystery, and nervous about what might be waiting deeper in the forest.

Sam knew exactly where we were headed. She clearly knew the woods better than I did, and loved them just as much as I did.

As we ran, I thought about how quickly I had gotten used to my new, weird life.

In fantasy books like Harry Potter, people just seem to go with the flow. "Turns out I'm a wizard, and everything I thought I knew about the world is wrong? Oh, okay." They take it really easily, and I always thought that was unrealistic.

But it turns out that's the way it is in real life. When the world turns out to be different than you thought, you can either accept it or fight it. And when the evidence is staring you in the face, you pretty much have to accept it or live a lie.

Talking animals? Okay. Let's roll with it. What other option is there?

Was I shocked? Was this weird and life-changing? Of course. But I was going with it.

We came up to the old rail car before long, panting and out of breath.

What we saw didn't really solve any of our mysteries.

If anything, it gave us more.

The rusty blue car was wide open, as always, but the clearing had used to be clean. There hadn't been so much as a plastic bag before.

Now there was an old generator, and wires and speakers littered the ground in a haphazard arrangement.

We made our way closer, and I started to notice that there was a pattern. The speakers weren't just thrown here: they were all placed upright, facing different directions and scattered around, but clearly placed carefully.

And something else seemed off about the arrangement.

Sam and I went to different sides of the car, but we didn't see anything other than more speakers. We traced a couple of wires, and found they all connected to one stereo system, which was connected to the generator.

Definitely not just tossed here.

Someone had been using this sound system. But why out here in the middle of nowhere? If it had been a party thrown by some teenagers, there would have been all sorts of trash, like broken bottles and crushed cups and who knows what else. But the clearing was completely clean except for the speakers and wires.

Inside the stereo was an old, unmarked cassette tape. I wondered what was on it, but I didn't know anyone with a cassette player. I wasn't even sure how it worked. And we could never lug this monstrosity back home. That would have been a conversation.

"Hey Mom, brought home a giant cassette player from the woods. Don't know why I'd ever want it, but I dragged it home just the same."

Sam and I stood side by side and watched Basset sniff around.

"Anything?" I asked.

"Not really," he said. "A few bugs, and a human-type scent but I've never smelled it before."

"Just one?"

He sniffed around a bit more.

"Definitely. One person. Sorry buddy, but I don't smell anything else."

"I'm not noticing something," Sam said. "Something's wrong here."

"I know," I said. "I get the same feeling. But what are we missing?"

We kept looking around. The speakers were all different sizes, and they were all caked in mud and leaves.

"It's definitely weird," Sam said. "A surround sound system in the woods, but it doesn't really explain anything, does it?"

"I wish weasels could be a little more direct," I said.

"We all do," Basset responded with a sigh.

Suddenly Sam straightened up, like she had noticed something.

"They're new," she said slowly.

"What?"

"The speakers. They're all new."

She ran up to one of the larger speakers and brushed off the mud. Underneath, the plastic was in great shape.

She ran up to another, and then another. Different sizes and different companies, but they were all brand new.

Then I remembered something from this morning. Something that I hadn't really paid attention to, but it was slowly coming back to me. Like someone walking closer through the fog, it was coming clearer.

"Someone bought thousands of dollars' worth of sound equipment and dumped them in a muddy clearing?" Sam asked.

"Just one more thing to add to our 'weird crap in the woods' list," I said, but I wasn't really paying attention. I kept staring off into the distance, trying to coax that memory out of the fog.

Speakers. Sound equipment.

Of course! It was obvious now, but when you're only half paying attention it's hard to remember something.

That's one thing I learned in school.

"Sam, have you heard of the Masked Marauder?"

"Ummm, I think so," she said slowly. "Some burglar or something? I don't really pay attention to the newspaper, but I've heard people talking."

"Me too. But I saw something in the paper my dad was reading this morning. Just glanced at it, but if I'm remembering right, the headline said something about the Masked Marauder robbing an electronics store."

"Seriously? So this is all stolen? Jeez, it must have taken a thousand hands to grab all of this stuff."

"Yeah, he's supposed to be good at stealing lots of things at once, I think."

"Well now we know *who* put all this stuff here, but we still don't know why."

"Masked Marauder's really embarrassed about his musical tastes and needs a private party-spot?"

Basset was back sniffing around, and he was now near the generator.

He had picked something interesting up, I could tell.

"What is it boy?"

"Gas." He said. He sniffed up and down the generator. "I think this thing still has some gas in it."

"It still has gas in it?" I asked, not sure I got his point.

"So we can crank it up and see what these speakers were

playing!" Sam said, excitedly running over to the generator.

She yanked the cord, and the generator came to life with a sputter and a cough.

I went over to the stereo.

"Okay, so I'm guessing it works just like an iPad," I said. "There's a play button. Let's see what happens."

I hit the button, the tape started to go, but no sound came out.

As soon as I hit the button, Basset went running into the woods. That was nothing unusual; he probably smelled a squirrel. But I thought he had enough self-control to stay and find out what was on the tape.

We kept listening for a couple of seconds, but there was still no sound.

I hit the fast-forward and rewind buttons, stopping every few seconds to listen again. It was blank.

"Weird," Sam said.

I finally turned it off.

Looked like the investigation had come to a close.

Out of the corner of my eye, I saw Basset returning – slowly, very slowly – and with a scared look on his face.

He kept looking from one side to the other, like he was worried a bear was about to leap out of the woods at any moment.

"What is it boy?" I asked, running up to him. I was definitely worried.

"Is it gone? Is it coming back, you think?"

"What boy? What did you see?"

"You mean – you mean you didn't hear it?"

"Hear what? What was it boy?"

"The screaming. That awful, evil, terrible screaming."

Sam nodded, and then bent down to pet Basset's back.

"It's okay now boy, the sound isn't coming back," she said.

"How can you know that?" Basset asked.

"Yeah, how do you know Sam? We didn't even hear it."

"Of course not," she said. "It was too high pitched for us to hear. Like a dog whistle. Whatever was on that tape could only be heard by certain animals."

Basset got that "I got into the trash and I'm so sorry" look on his face again.

"You mean, it was just on that tape?"

"I guess so boy," I said, scratching him behind the ears. "It's not your fault; you didn't know it was just a recording."

"I'm supposed to protect you," Basset said, that look getting worse on his face. "I'm supposed to get between you and trouble, not run away from it."

"Thanks buddy. I'd do the same for you. But it's okay, it was just a tape. You didn't need to protect me from that."

"Yeah. This time."

I patted him one more time, and then stood up.

"So it's a sound only animals can hear," I said. "It sounds so crazy I almost don't want to say it, but..." I trailed off.

Sam picked right up where I had stopped: "...but the Masked Marauder used the tape to scare all the birds out of the woods."

I nodded.

"But why?" I asked. "Why would anyone steal all this equipment and drag it all the way out here and go through all this trouble just to scare off some crows and sparrows?"

"I don't know," Basset said. "But it's not good."

"Not good at all," I agreed. "Something's going on here, and it means trouble."

Chapter 13

THE FIRST CLUE

Before we left, I decided to take one last look around, although I didn't know what I hoped to find.

I checked all the speakers, checked inside the stereo, and even checked in the train car to see if there was anything unusual. But there was nothing.

Finally I went over to the generator to turn it off.

As I was looking for the switch, something caught my eye.

There was a little piece of plastic sticking out of a crack in the machine.

I switched the generator off and grabbed the edge.

It was tiny, just a half an inch sticking out and very thin, like the very edge of a credit card, but it was wedged in there good.

I pulled and wiggled, and finally more of it came out.

It looked like it might have *been* a credit card, but the heat from the machine had melted it and made it bubble up all over the place.

It had started off white, and was now marked all over with brown and black burn marks.

There were no words I could read, just a couple of blurry letters I could make out: "G---- Co--- Lib----"

I stared harder at it, but couldn't make out the other letters.

They were too blurred from the scorch marks.

I showed it to Sam, and then to Basset.

"What do you think it is?" I asked.

"Looks like an ID, a driver's license or something," Sam said.

"I'm a little out of my element here, buddy," Basset said. "I can't read."

That's something most people don't know about dogs: almost all of them are dyslexic.

They also don't have schools.

Or hands to write with.

Or to hold books with.

Reading's pretty tough for them, is what I'm getting at.

"It's late," Sam said. "I gotta get back before my old man gets home."

"Yeah, we should be heading back too," I said. "My parents hate it if I'm late for dinner."

I put the card in my pocket and we made our way through the woods, but I couldn't stop pulling the card back out to stare at it.

Maybe if I squinted hard enough I could read it.

This had to be the key. An ID would tell us exactly who the Masked Marauder was, and then we could turn him in and find out why he'd gotten rid of the birds. And how to get them back.

Whatever he was planning we could foil it.

G---- Co--- Lib----.

Something kept tickling the back of my brain. Something I didn't want to recognize for some reason.

Then it hit me: "Guster Cooper Liberman."

He had been bragging all last week that he had gotten a fake ID. It was a good one too, looked just like a real driver's license.

He wasn't too bright though. It said his age was 17. So, sure, it made him look older, but not old enough to *do* anything. What, he wanted to drive his nonexistent car? I don't know many 13-year-olds who make enough money from their allowance (or from stealing some middle school lunch money) to buy a car.

Unless Brussels sprout breath is an acceptable form of payment now.

So his ID wouldn't get him any drinking or smoking or gambling.

He was just showing off his lack of foresight.

I kept this suspicion to myself. For now at least.

Was Guster really smart enough to rig up a sound system like that?

I knew he hated birds. He couldn't stand their singing and whistling, and liked to fire at them with his slingshot. He loved to torture animals in general, such as burning ants with his trusty magnifying glass.

But he wasn't clever enough, was he?

I needed more evidence before I brought this up to Sam or Basset. I didn't want them to think that I was just trying to get revenge on my bully.

I didn't think I was. Was I? Sure, I was biased, but the card looked exactly like his fake ID, and the letters I could see were an *exact* match for the letters in his name.

I was excited. I was almost positive I had figured it out.

I just needed more evidence.

Chapter 14
THE LAST DINNER

As we were eating dinner that night (Chinese takeout instead of pizza this time), I asked my dad if I could read the paper.

He looked surprised, but then gave me a proud look.

"Taking a bit more of an interest in current events, eh? Glad to see it. Look champ, you know I love you, but you fill your head with too many silly books sometimes. It's frivolous. This," he tapped the paper, "this is important stuff. Not what some dorky man-witch is up to in his castle fighting bad guys with no name."

I didn't bother telling him that Harry Potter is a wizard, not a witch. He wouldn't care about something so "frivolous." Stories about the county zoning board or stories telling everyone that it is currently summertime and outdoor activities exist; *that's* important stuff.

I immediately turned to the front page and the article about the Masked Marauder.

The more I read, the more I was convinced that he was the one responsible for chasing away the birds. I still had no idea *why* anyone would want to get rid of birds, but he was clearly involved.

He stole 57 speakers of different sizes, a stereo, and a generator. Police couldn't figure out how he loaded a 200-pound generator and all that equipment into his getaway vehicle in the half-hour the security guard was away on his break.

It was weird.

Then again, everything else about the Masked Marauder was weird.

For instance, no one had seen him. Not a security camera, not a random person on the street, no one.

Which made me wonder why they named him the "Masked" anything if no one had seen a mask. But that was answered a little later in the story.

It was what he called *himself*.

At every crime scene he'd left a note taking responsibility for the burglary. He clearly wanted attention.

What was even weirder was that the notes were written on some kind of soft, thick paper, almost like a silk napkin.

I didn't know Guster had so much class.

"Hey Mom, what do Mr. and Mrs. Liberman do for work?" I asked casually while reading the story.

"Why do you want to know sweetie?"

"Just trying to get to know the neighborhood kids better. Nothing special."

My mom sounded happy. "Oh, well in that case, your new friend's parents own a store downtown. Something to do with house wares."

"It's kitchen and dining room stuff," my dad corrected. "You know: china, silverware, napkins, that sort of thing."

Well that answered that.

"Kitchen and dining room 'stuff' *is* house wares," my mom said. "Those rooms are in the house. That's why they call it *house* wares."

"I was just trying to be more specific. Give the boy the most accurate information. That's the key."

I didn't want the "definition of house wares" battle to turn into a full-scale war. I could tell what an important topic this was, but I wasn't sure it warranted a heated debate.

"So they own a store? That's interesting," I said, trying to change the subject.

"Yes honey," my mom said, shooting my dad a look and then turning back to me. "Do you want me to invite the Libermans over for dinner sometime next week?"

I almost choked on my fortune cookie, which would have been UNfortunate.

Sorry. Bad pun.

I held my cough in, drank some water, and tried not to show the horror in my eyes.

"No, that's okay, Mom. I don't want you to trouble yourself with having to cook a big meal."

"I think that's a good idea," my dad said.

"Right," I said quickly, before my mom could take offense. "Maybe some other time."

Like maybe after Guster is dragged to juvenile hall, I thought.

I went back to reading the paper. There wasn't a lot more that seemed interesting in the story.

The Marauder had robbed a lumberyard, a comic book store, a pet store, and the local museum. It seemed awfully random. At the museum he stole some old artifacts from the Native American exhibit (it said it was the Lakota tribe) that weren't worth a lot of money. In fact, nothing that he stole was worth that much. And it didn't seem to have any connection.

Unless he was building a house for a group of comics-loving puppies I couldn't figure out why he'd rob those first three stores. And that of course made no sense.

Dogs are colorblind.

After a while I decided that I couldn't get any more out of

the paper. I pretended to read a few articles ("War in the Middle East" and "Is your bathtub a deathtrap?") and then said I was heading up to my room early because I wanted to get up at dawn to play with a new friend.

"Oh, is it that Liberman boy?" my mom asked.

"No, I don't think you know her," I responded. "Anyway, goodnight!"

The paper definitely pointed to Guster. I didn't know *why* he was doing all this weird, illegal stuff, but it had to be him.

This still wasn't proof though.

If only I could find someone who could read that ID card.

I started to make my way up the stairs to my room when I thought I heard more scuffling noises from behind the crawlspace door. I bent down and put my ear against the rough wood, and listened.

There was nothing for a while, the seconds dragging by slowly, but then I heard it again: a ticking.

Not like a clock. It was really fast, like a metronome turned up as high as it will go, or a thousand tiny drummers playing heavy metal.

I *had* to see what was behind the door.

I tried the locks, but even though they were rusty they were solid.

I took a closer look at them.

They looked like they all had the same key, but there were no old keys lying around the house when we moved in. I did a full exploration of the house on the first weekend after the move, looking for any cool items the previous owners left behind.

No such luck.

The locks looked simple, like they could easily be picked, but I had no idea how to do that.

In movies they just stick a needle in there, wiggle it around, and the lock magically pops open.

It's not that easy in real life.

Believe me. I've tried.

I tugged on one of the locks and the ticking stopped.

I tried to look under the door, but it was too close to the floor to see anything.

There was an old keyhole too, but it had been filled in with plaster.

Someone really wanted to keep people from looking in.

Or some *thing* from looking out.

I didn't want to give up. It's like when I got a bike for Christmas but had to wait three days for my dad to put it together, or when there was a new book at the library but it was already checked out. I wanted to go in there *now* and find out what was making that noise.

But I couldn't.

So I sucked it up and went up to my room, where Basset was waiting for me on the bed.

"So what do you think we should do tomorrow?" I asked.

"I'm still thinking it over. We have to figure out what's going on here and make sure the birds are okay, but I don't know where to start. Listen Nate, you don't think this is dangerous, do you?"

"Not really, no."

"Good. Because I don't want you poking your nose into anything that could get you hurt. Bad things can pop out of holes. I've poked MY nose in enough porcupine burrows to know that."

"I know you're worried about me buddy. But I don't think we're up against some criminal mastermind here. And we've got Sam. No one in their right mind would mess with her."

"That's a good point. She's incredibly tall."

I laughed. "She sure is."

I thought for a few seconds. "Do you know anyone in the neighborhood who can help us read the letters on the ID card?"

"Hmmm…" he thought for a good long while. "I can't think of anyone. I could take it to Douglas the hound. He's got a great nose, even better than mine, but I don't think it would do any good. All you can smell on it is gasoline. And I don't know anyone with great eyesight. Dogs and cats can't see as well as humans."

"I know…."

I took a few more seconds.

"I guess some birds have great eyesight. We were learning about it in school."

"They sure do. Especially birds of prey."

"That's right! Hawks and falcons, they use their eyes to hunt. I mean, birds eat spiders and stuff, so they *have* to see super well."

"One problem though: all the birds are gone."

"Yeah, I noticed."

I laughed, but it quickly faltered. This wasn't really a funny situation.

"So no one can help us read it?" I asked.

"Not that I can think of…"

I knew this wasn't Guster's reason for getting rid of the birds. There was no way he could know I could talk to animals, or that I would need their help in reading a burnt up ID card he hadn't even dropped yet.

But it was a frustrating coincidence. The only people who could help us figure out why the birds disappeared were the birds.

Not super helpful.

We chatted a bit more, about how awesome Sam's fort was, about what else might be hidden away in those woods, what other forgotten places and mysteries were out there. I talked about how much fun it would be to read in the fort, away from parents who think fantasy books are "nonsense" because you should only read schoolbooks or the newspaper.

We eventually settled down to sleep without getting any further in our investigation. I had no idea where to go from there.

As I tried to sleep, I couldn't get my dad's words out of my mind. The books I read were "frivolous."

It wasn't the substance of his opinion that bugged me so much. It was the dismissive way he had *given* his opinion. Like it wasn't even a conversation. Like his opinion was obviously right, and I was just too young to understand it yet. But when I grow up I'll see that imagination is a waste of time, right?

That's one thing I can't stand about adults: they treat us like kids. Well, we are kids, but I mean they treat us like *young* kids. They completely forget what it's like to be our age. Our section of the library is called "Young Adult," but our parents only see the first half.

I'm not saying I don't respect my parents. I obey them, usually without questioning, because I know they've been around longer and know more than I do about a lot of things. I get that. There's a lot I don't know.

But here's the thing: there's a lot I *do* know.

I respect my parents. I just wish they respected me a bit more.

You know what I'm talking about. Why do so many adults treat 13-year-olds the exact same way they treat 3-year-olds? Like we can't understand anything, like our minds are too simple to grasp "adult" concepts.

I don't know about you, but I'm a lot further along than when I was 3. For one thing, I can read.

For another, I have the ability to think and reason and hold conversations that don't just circle around topics like "how's school?" and "what do you want to be when you grow up?"

We're expected to learn advanced math and language and poetry, but they can't talk to us like adults.

I'm not saying a 13-year-old should be able to drive a car. I'm just saying they could treat us like we can think for ourselves. Because we can, right?

Have adults really forgotten that much about being our age? Is it just one big blur? You're either a kid or an adult, and there's no in between? From our perspective, it's a long road to adulthood, and we're well into the journey. We compare ourselves to what we were, and we've grown. Adults don't see it. They just see "kid," like we're all the same.

We might look young to them, but we look pretty mature to ourselves. Because this is as mature as we've ever been. We can't compare it to adulthood, because we haven't been there yet.

How can they expect us to learn to act respectably if we can't earn their respect?

I feel bad about thinking these things now because of what happened next: my parents disappeared.

Chapter 15
THE PHANTOM RETURNS

In the middle of the night I had the dream again.

I "woke up" drenched in freezing sweat that made my skin tingle, my heart galloping.

Basset was gone.

The death-white mask stared at me through the window.

I tried to tell myself that it was just a dream, but I couldn't shake the terror I felt. Like when you're in line to a roller coaster and you try to calm yourself down and tell yourself there's nothing *rational* to be scared of. But your emotions don't always listen to reason.

Once again, it felt more real than any dream I'd ever had, but this time I figured it *had* to be a dream. I mean, I'd just read about the Masked Marauder right before I went to bed, and now a masked man was floating in front of my window?

Obviously a dream.

Still frozen to my bed, I watched as the gloved hand reached up to the window.

The hand moved kind of like a puppet, all jerky and erratic. Like the bones were shivering.

The glove slowly scratched out words on my window again. Different words this time, but they made just as much sense as last time, as much sense as math class. That is to say: none at all.

"When the indoor sun is upside down

And the smile becomes a frown

Then the answers will appear

Never known to be so near."

This time it rhymed.

Well that was new.

"What the heck does that mean?" I asked out loud. It can't hurt to ask your dreams what they mean, even if they almost never answer.

The mask kept staring at me, not moving an inch.

The moon came out from behind a cloud, shining cold white light on everything, but I still couldn't make out much of the person's body, or how he was hovering in front of the second story window.

Just more evidence of this being a dream.

The mask almost seemed to twinkle or glow in the moonlight, as if covered in strands of silver.

Then, in the blink of an eye, it was gone.

Basset hadn't returned yet, but I settled back into bed nonetheless.

He'd be there when I woke up.

Just like normal.

Chapter 16
THE RIDDLE

He was there.

But it wasn't normal.

For the second day in a row I found Basset sitting by the window, staring out with that inexplicable sad look.

"Still worried about the birds?" I asked as I got up.

"Certainly. But that's not what I'm looking at now."

I lifted my eyes from Basset and looked out the window. I didn't see it for a second. It can be hard to see things when they're right in front of your eyes.

The words.

They were still there.

The words the dream phantom had scribbled on the window were still there.

Dreams don't usually do that.

"You didn't see anything last night, did you?" he asked. "I can't figure how someone could have written this up here without a ladder, and that would've woken me up for sure."

"I...I thought that was a dream!"

"You saw something?"

I told him about everything. About my first dream and the one last night, about the phantom's jerky movements and the death

91

mask. I read him the note, but he had no more ideas about it than I did.

"Why didn't you wake me?" Basset asked, sounding kind of hurt.

"I thought it was a dream. Besides, you weren't here."

"Oh my." He paused. "I smelled the oddest smell late last night, like nothing I've ever smelled before, and went downstairs to investigate. Nothing. But when I got back you were still sound asleep just as I left you. I never would have gone if I'd known there was an intruder outside."

"It's okay boy. You didn't know. Besides, it's not like he did anything. Words can't hurt you."

I laughed to try and break the tense feeling in the room, but it didn't quite do the trick.

This was just too weird.

"Do you smell anything now? Any clues as to who left this?"

"Believe me, I've tried. There's nothing. Not even the slightest scent. Everything as it should be."

We sat for a couple more seconds in silence, but sitting still wouldn't solve much of anything.

We needed to get out and see Sam. She might have a better idea of what the clues meant.

I raced downstairs, not even pausing as I heard more ticking behind the crawlspace door.

"Someone's in quite a rush this morning!" my mom said as she was pouring out the soggy remnants of her cereal.

"Beautiful day!" I responded, snatching a granola bar. "Friend of mine wants to play out in the woods."

"A friend?" my dad asked, that proud look he got when I picked up the paper last night returning to his eyes. "Glad to hear it. You spend too much time locked up alone in that room of yours with your books."

I somehow managed to keep my eyes from rolling. It kind of hurt.

I didn't mention that I planned on reading some extremely frivolous books with my new friend. You know, after our current disappearing-birds-and-floating-death-faces investigation was over.

"Who is he?" my mom asked.

"Name's Sam," I said quickly. "Didn't get her last name. Lives on Maple. Gotta go!"

As I raced out the back door I heard my dad shout after me "We'll have to talk later!"

Not sure what that was about, but I didn't stop to think about it. The woods waited.

We made our way to the fort in short order, and found Sam already there waiting for us.

"I'm glad you came back," she said. Her shyness had returned.

"Of course I came back. This place is awesome. Besides, we need your help in figuring all this out."

She relaxed and beamed at me.

"Great. Okay, I've been thinking. We need to search for more clues, but we also need to make sense of the clues we already have. We have to find a way to read that ID."

"Agreed," I nodded. "So where do we start?"

"I'm not sure. My dad's got a magnifying glass at home. If I wait until he goes to the worksite I can sneak back and grab it for a couple hours."

"That's a good idea. The letters are there, they're just too worn down to read without getting a closer look."

"It might take me a bit to snatch the magnifying glass, and my dad would think it's suspicious if you were hanging around the house. So you wanna hang out here while I'm out?"

"I want to be more help than that," I said thoughtfully. I wasn't sure what I could do. "Hey! Why don't I go down to the library? I'm sure there's books there that talk about which animals have the best eyesight, and if we can find one maybe one of them can read it."

"That's a great idea. Let's meet back here a little after lunchtime."

Chapter 17

THE LIBRARY

It was agreed. While Sam made her way back home I took a shortcut through the woods to downtown.

Our village downtown wasn't anything special: a bank, two churches, a comics and "novelties" store, a handful of restaurants, and the library. Adults called it "cute" and "quaint," but for us kids it was just "boring."

On my way to the library, I saw Mr. Mulligan making his way up the street towards me, but before I could duck away he spotted me.

Mr. Mulligan was one of those adults who thinks he's great with kids, but honestly doesn't know the difference between a 13-year-old and a 3 year old. Or a 13-year-old and a puppy for that matter. Most of the village parents knew him, and none of them liked him too much. He was not very friendly to adults, kind of gruff and self-centered, and a definite stickler for the rules.

He was in charge of the neighborhood watch, and would hand out tickets for every little crime, no matter how small. "You parked your car facing the wrong way. Better not let me catch you doing that again." "I noticed your porch light was on after 10 p.m. We don't live in a lawless land, you know."

The parents *did* like that he was so nice to the kids. He was always giving us lollipops and candies and treats, but he didn't treat us much like people. I always got the sense he kept candies in his pocket for the same reason a mailman might keep dog treats with him: because he's scared, and wants to distract the vermin in case he has to make a hasty getaway.

But he only pulled out the candy at the end of his conversations. He always talked our ears off, probably because none of the adults wanted to talk to him. You know, because he might ticket them for using the wrong word. So he'd give us a nice long rambling speech about how his job was annoying and his leg was acting up and no one around here appreciated his neighborhood watch program.

It was always awkward running into him.

"Hey there buddy!" he shouted like he'd spotted a puppy. "Have you been a good boy? How's school going?" He never gave us a chance to answer. "Going good, huh? Bet you're learning all sorts of fun stuff, like how to read and write?"

I prayed under my breath that this would be over soon.

"I saw your dad the other day down at the store, and I said to him 'boy, it'd sure be nice to have a job like yours. I saw your house lights on until after midnight last night. Must be nice to go into work whenever you want.'"

I didn't know how to respond to that. Did I defend my dad and tell Mr. Mulligan that Dad works very hard and wakes up at the crack of dawn every morning, and Mr. Mulligan should give people their freaking privacy? Or did I just keep my mouth shut? Arguing with Mr. Mulligan would just make the conversation last longer.

I didn't even get a chance to decide.

"Well he nodded at me like he knew what I meant. Everyone around here knows what a thankless job I do down at the plant." He shook his head sadly. "Everyone knows."

"Oh, I think everyone knows about your job alright. They're always talking about it." Luckily he missed the sarcasm and didn't skip a beat.

"Certainly. I'm sure it's the talk of the town."

This was getting painful.

"Anywho, I'd better get running. The neighborhood doesn't watch itself. Here. Have a butterscotch."

I didn't bother asking what crimes he expected to happen in our neighborhood at 10 a.m. A heist of Mrs. Marple's pies? A gang of well-equipped bank robbers stealing a whopping 10 dollars and 44 cents from Mr. Bondangle's store? Or (gasp!) a lunatic parking his car facing the wrong way?!

I also didn't bother telling him butterscotch reminded me of old ladies.

Didn't want to hurt his feelings, after all.

Mercifully he walked away and I continued straight on into the library.

I spotted Mr. Barston behind the old wooden librarian's desk and broke into a smile. He was always my favorite librarian. He loved chatting about books with everyone, especially the kids because we were "still discovering the wonders of reading."

He was definitely more friendly than the standard "shushing and be quietly stern" librarians.

"Good morning master Nate," he said, tipping his cap at me. "What brings you in here today?"

"Well sir, I found a wallet on the ground outside, but I couldn't read the ID inside to find out whose it is," I said, handing him the card. I felt bad lying, but "I suspect my school bully is part of a plot to chase away birds using stolen stereo equipment while calling himself the Masked Marauder" wasn't really something I wanted to say out loud to too many people.

"And you were hoping one of our books might prove

useful in deciphering the writing," Mr. Barston said with a nod as he thoughtfully looked at the card. "Unfortunately, I seem to have left my glasses at home this morning, so I'm afraid I won't be much help to you myself. But we have some wonderful books on magnification and other investigation techniques."

He pointed me in the right direction and I walked straight over there. I didn't pick up a single book though. Magnification was Sam's job. My job was to research animals.

Once I was out of sight I headed over to the nature section.

I picked up anatomy books specializing in eyesight, books on animals that are particularly good at hunting, and books on nocturnal hunters. None of them proved very useful.

Chameleon's have amazing eyesight, apparently. They can look in two directions at once and can spot tiny insects moving incredibly quickly, but where was I going to find a chameleon in the suburbs?

There was also an animal called the tarsier, but I didn't read much about it. If I'd never even heard of it, chances are it doesn't live around here.

Colossal squid and four eyed fish have some incredible eyes, but I didn't feel like heading out to the ocean, diving down a mile underwater, and trying to decipher the blubs of sealife.

The last animal I found that fit my criteria was the ogre faced spider. That sounded terrifying. Even if bugs *could* talk, I wasn't sure I'd want to go hunting for a spider with a name like "ogre faced."

I of course ran across tons of books mentioning hawks and falcons, but the birds were all gone.

The library looked like a bust.

Chapter 18
DECIPHERING THE RIDDLE

I was pretty discouraged as I made my way back to the fort, and felt like I had wasted a solid hour and a half, but I cheered myself up by reminding myself that Sam was on her way with a magnifying glass.

When I opened the heavy oak door of the fort, I found Sam sitting at the table with the exact same look of defeat on her face.

She looked up at me and said "You too, huh? No luck?"

I shook my head and sat next to her. "Nada. But what happened with you? Where's the magnifying glass?"

"My old man left for the worksite exactly when I thought he would, and I snuck into his room and grabbed the magnifying glass. Easy as pie, just as I suspected. But as I was reaching for the doorknob to go outside, my dad burst back in. He forgot his lunch or something. Anyway, long story short, I'm grounded for two weeks and I don't have anything to show for it."

"Man, I'm sorry."

"It's not your fault. It doesn't really matter anyway. He's not around to make sure I'm staying grounded, and he'll probably forget all about it by tonight. I'm just sorry we can't solve this clue because my dad is such a pain in the butt about his stuff."

I slumped back in my chair. Where did we go from here?

I wanted to cheer Sam up, or at least give us something to take our minds off the morning's failure.

"Listen, we might have another clue already," I said slowly. "Not that it makes any sense."

I told her all about my "dreams" and the note we found this morning.

"Death is coming. Look in Baskertonn Manor. 2 1 18 19 20 15 14."

And, "When the indoor sun is upside down, And the smile becomes a frown, Then the answers will appear, Never known to be so near."

"Well that's super helpful."

I figured she was being sarcastic. I would have been.

"I know. It doesn't get us one single step further."

"I was serious," Sam said with a laugh. "Not the second one. I don't get any of that poetry gibberish. But the first one. Baskertonn Manor. That's where we need to start."

"But no one knows where it is. No person in this town has seen it in decades. It's just a story."

"It's out there in the woods somewhere. You're right, no *person* has seen the old house. But I'm sure some of the animals know where it is."

I can't believe I didn't think of that.

Then again, I never claimed to be a genius.

Some days I'm lucky I can remember how to tie my shoes.

"Jeez. You work fast."

"It's nothing special."

"Sure it is. I had that clue a week ago and didn't get as far as you did in two seconds."

"Anyway, where should we start?" She was looking at

Basset.

"Not with Genevieve this time, I'm guessing," I said. "Might as well ask a fish to tell us what it's like to fly. That cat's as domesticated as they come."

"Look, I'm not sure where to start this time around," Basset said slowly. "I don't know a ton of the forest animals. They tend to keep to themselves."

"Why don't we ask the squirrels?" Sam asked. "Those guys are *everywhere*. And they must talk to each other. I'm always hearing them chatter away."

"Oh they chatter alright," I said. "You're lucky you can't understand them. It's like listening to an even ruder Jim Carrey on fast forward."

I laughed, but Basset didn't seem amused.

"I was afraid it would come to that," he sighed. "She's right. No one knows the woods like them."

"Okay then," Sam clapped her hands together once excitedly. "Let's do this! We're really getting somewhere."

Basset looked embarrassed.

"It's not that easy," I said. "Basset and the squirrels, they don't get along super well."

"Yeah, he doesn't seem like the kind of dog who cares much for annoying rude animals. He's too smart for that." Sam patted Basset on the head, and Basset looked up at her with his tongue hanging out and his tail wagging.

"Okay, now I *really* like this kid," Basset said.

I laughed and told Sam.

"It's the truth. You're too sophisticated for it." She paused. "But let's not embarrass you too much. So where *do* we start?"

Basset sighed again. "If there's really no other way, absolutely no other way, we should talk to Franklin. He and the squirrels get along swimmingly."

"Who's Franklin?" Sam asked.

"He's the puggle a couple houses down from you on Maple," I responded. "He's an...excitable little guy. Not a lot better than the squirrels, honestly."

"Of course he is," Basset said with a completely straight face. "He doesn't hurl nuts at me."

I laughed but hugged Basset. I knew he didn't find this funny.

"Well what are we waiting for?" Sam asked.

And with that we headed out of the fort, not realizing that at that very minute my life was about to change forever, and my parents had suddenly disappeared.

Chapter 19
MEETING THE SQUIRRELS

We made our way down Maple Avenue, which, ironically, didn't have a single maple along it.

Politicians aren't great at coming up with street names.

And yes, I'm pretty sure I used the word ironically right.

Franklin was standing under a giant elm (by the way: no elms on Elm Street), looking up into the branches and shaking his tail so hard his pudgy backside was swinging side to side.

Franklin got his name because his owners said he looked like Benjamin Franklin. I didn't see it. I thought he looked like that actor, Steve Buscemi.

"Hey guys guess what there's a thing up in that tree that I don't know what it is but it's really cool and I need to get it."

Talking to other dogs always reminded me how lucky I was to have Basset. Most dogs can't calm themselves down as well as Basset can. And I know it's hard for him. He's willing to make the sacrifice.

"Hey Franklin. Who's a good boy?" I said as I walked up to him and started petting both of his droopy jowls.

Sam joined me and scratched Franklin's belly when he rolled onto his back.

"You're such a cute little guy," Sam said.

Franklin was almost too happy for words by this point.

"Oh boy oh boy oh boy oh boy," he kept saying over and over again. His tail was a blur and was hitting the ground every time he said "oh boy" like it was a drummer keeping time.

I don't know if you've ever met a puggle, but they're some of the ugliest and at the same time cutest dogs you'll ever see. They also *love* human attention. I've seen one get its tail stuck in a fence gate, and when he saw me approaching he couldn't help from trying to wag it. The entire back half of the dog started wagging instead.

After a few seconds Sam and I back off, and Franklin jumped to his feet, panting away and staring at us.

We had grabbed his attention from "the thing in the tree."

"Franklin, you haven't seen any squirrels around today, have you?" I asked trying to sound casual.

It didn't work.

"You need my help? Oh boy I love helping almost as much as I love my food and love digging and love playing with squirrels and –"

"That's great Franklin. Now, have you seen any squirrels today?"

"I sure have! Oh! There was also this smell earlier, something like garbage and grass mixed. It was *so* awesome!"

"Fantastic. Where did you see the squirrel?"

"That's when I saw the thing in the tree and I think it's a Frisbee or a ball or something I can play with I just *know* it is."

Great.

Back to the thing in the tree.

It's hard to get a dog to focus.

But you have to stay patient. Otherwise he'll just apologize. A lot.

Sam, as usual, had the solution, even though she could only

hear my half of the conversation.

"Franklin? Hey buddy? You wanna help us out?" She matched Franklin's energy and got the dog excited to help. "Can you chase down a squirrel for us so we can all play in the yard together?"

"Oh boy a big play I'll be right back!"

And with that the dog whizzed away into the woods. You wouldn't think a waddling dog like that could whiz, but he sure could. It was a waddle in fast forward. A whiz waddle. A wazzle, if you will.

"You did it again," I said to Sam while we waited for Franklin to come back. "You're really good with animals you know."

Sam looked nervous, and grimaced slightly like her stomach was upset. "I'm not sure...you know I just notice things."

"No, it's more than that. You really have a way with them. You're even better at communicating with animals than I am, and I can actually hear them," I laughed and shook my head in disbelief.

"I love animals," she said, with a kind of distant and faraway look in her eyes. "But I don't think I'm good with them."

I was about to ask her what she meant, but at that moment Franklin returned, with a whole posse of squirrels chattering behind him.

Basset looked up at me nervously.

"It's okay boy. You can do it," I whispered.

"You won't listen to any of the things they say, will you? I mean, they can be mean."

"You don't believe any of the nasty things Guster says about me, do you?"

"I don't think you're a pencil-necked-skeleton-nerd, no."

"I don't think a few squirrels can change my mind about you."

Basset looked a little relieved, but he was still nervous.

The squirrels started their barrage of wisecracks.

"Franklin the fatty."

"Pudgy puggle."

"Ha ha I guess I am a little soft in the middle but thanks for coming with me I love playing."

"You're too slow to do much playing."

"More like wandering aimlessly."

"We love playing with you." The tone of voice said "playing with" like he meant "teasing."

Franklin didn't notice.

"I love it when we play because running is the best almost as best as eating and almost as best as getting my tummy rubbed."

Franklin was too friendly to understand when he was being made fun of. Sometimes it seemed sad, but usually I envied him. He wasn't stupid. He just didn't want to see bad in others and instead chose to be happy and have fun no matter what.

I know it's dangerous to ignore the evil that's in the world. But sometimes his upbeat attitude seemed so right. Like he wasn't ignoring the evil, just dealing with it by not letting it affect his life.

That's when the squirrels noticed Basset.

"You didn't say it was *Basset* who needed our help," one squirrel said while racing into the elm tree.

They all started chattering away one right after the other as they jumped into the branches, like a machine gun of words.

"He's too slow to listen to us."

"Too fuzzy-headed more like."

"Head full of crap."

"Well he sniffs his own butt enough."

"And the butts of other dogs."

"You're filthy Basset."

"Serious flatulence problem too."

"Basset the gas it."

"Dog the hog."

"Canine the swine."

The squirrels started laughing all at once, which is a sound I'm sure you're familiar with. It's the nasty jabbering sound they make constantly.

Basset looked up at me sadly.

"Oh, sorry," I said, looking up at the squirrels. "Was I supposed to be listening to you? I don't usually pay much attention to rats."

The squirrels hissed at me, which can be a terrifying noise if you've never heard it.

Like weasels, they have sharp teeth. But they're usually too chicken to bite.

Unlike chickens. Which is weird.

The squirrels quickly recovered though.

"Stupid boy."

"Can't tell the difference between a rat and a squirrel?" The tone was condescending, like mocking a three year old for not being able to read.

"Do you need your mommy to explain animals to you again?"

"I think I'm fine thanks," I said, casually sticking my hands in my pockets and looking bored. It's important when dealing with squirrels to act like they have no effect on you.

It drives them crazy.

"I thought squirrels were just rats with bushy tales."

They hissed again, and I didn't give them a chance to respond.

"But maybe I'm wrong. Maybe *rats* are just squirrels without all that gaudy decoration on their behinds."

I knew I wasn't really getting us very far in our goal, but I couldn't stand the way they were teasing Basset.

"Don't make us toss nuts at you."

"We're pretty good shots."

"Nuts? Boy, I'd better watch out. What's next? You gonna flick some corn at me? Toss a crumb of cheese in my eye? You do enough and I can make a salad."

There was silence for a minute, and then an acorn came sailing out of the tree and hit me square on the forehead. It hurt, but I wasn't going to let that show.

"I thought you said *nuts*. What am I supposed to do with that? I'm not a big acorn fan, thanks just the same."

Another one struck me on the chest. That didn't really hurt.

"Got any pecans up there? My mom's making a pie."

I laughed.

"Seriously though. We need your help."

"Why should we help *you*?"

"Basset's always chasing us up trees."

"And he drops the IQ of the entire neighborhood five points."

"And that *smell!*"

I put my hands back in my pockets. They looked dumbfounded that their words didn't hurt. Keeping silent was a far more effective weapon than a thousand perfectly crafted insults in this situation.

"Why help me? I guess you don't have to. But you should. Because if you don't, Basset here will make sure you never eat in this neighborhood again."

"How?" The word came down from above a dozen times, like an owl got confused about what he was supposed to say.

"He's a lot smarter than you give him credit for."

Basset looked up at me, kind of confused, but also grateful.

"You guys are awfully lazy, you know," I continued. "Do you even remember how to get food from the *wild?*"

Basset picked up on where I was going.

"Probably not. You spend most of your time stealing from Mrs. McGreedy's garden, or pilfering birdfeeders. Well, I could see to it that there's a dog at all of your favorite spots, forcing you to get your food *honestly*. Which you should be doing anyway. But you don't remember how."

"My guess is a handful of acorns won't get you through the winter. Of course, if dogs are so slow, you could always try to run past them. They are slow, right? Isn't that what you said?"

There was silence.

I knew they'd never admit they were wrong, but I waited patiently.

"What do you need?" one of them asked.

"See, that wasn't so hard! You know you'd get a lot further in life if you just acted with a little more respect." It was my turn to act condescending.

"And didn't rely on thievery for survival," Basset added.

I didn't want to push it too far though.

"We need to know where Baskertonn Manor is."

"Go explore the woods then."

"Unless you think you'll get lost."

"Or are too slow to find it."

"Or too stupid."

"Unlike some creatures around here, I have no problem admitting when I have a weakness. I don't know these woods. And I'm not fast enough to explore them all in such a short amount of time. We have a deal?"

Squirrels talk so fast and so high pitched it can be tough to keep up, but I was determined to do so. I knew they'd only give me instructions once, and then tell me they met their end of the bargain. If I couldn't understand them, that would be my problem, not theirs. I said they had to *tell* me, not that I had to *hear* them. Loopholes. Squirrels love them.

"Fine."

"Whatever."

"No fur off my tail."

"How can we give directions even a human can follow?"

"Go down to the brook."

"By the head rock."

"Follow it until the tree that fell over the water."

"Turn left."

"Over the hill."

"Turn left again."

"It's there."

"Got it?"

"Good."

"Great."

"Don't forget to turn right at the log though."

"After the brook of course."

"But before the hill."

"Got it?"

"Good."

They chattered up above, laughing as they quickly jumped away and scurried back into the woods.

They didn't think I'd be able to remember those complicated directions, but I had a secret weapon: Mrs. Maplewood.

Mrs. Maplewood talked *just* as fast as a squirrel, and twice as high pitched. She made me immune to annoyingness. I could keep up.

Basset sighed.

"Well that wasn't too bad," he said.

I laughed. "Sure. Stubbing your toe is better than getting it chewed off by a wolverine, but I'd still rather not stub my toe just the same."

"They're that bad, huh?" Sam said.

"They're worse." I laughed again. "But we got what we came for."

I told Sam the directions, but this time rearranging them into the correct order.

"Okay...I think I know which brook they're talking about, but I've never been much further than that," she said. "That's deep in the woods."

"We won't get lost though. Not with Basset's nose to guide us home."

"Definitely," Sam said, giving Basset a pat on the head.

And with that we were on our way to the mysterious Baskertonn Manor.

Chapter 20
WALKING INTO THE UNKNOWN

We made our way into the woods through my backyard, and after about a half hour of walking we made it to the brook.

Sam was right: it *was* deep in the woods. A lot deeper than I had ever gone. This forest must be massive, way bigger than the empty lot behind my parents' old house. We had walked probably two miles, and there was no end in sight.

That's a lot of forest for a suburban village.

We walked along the stream, and the gurgling, laughing water sounded really loud after the deep silence of the woods. Even this far in there wasn't a single bird. Not a tweet.

It took us another half hour to navigate the rest of the instructions, which were actually really accurate. Say what you want about the squirrels, but they stuck to their end of the bargain while trying to loophole us.

While we walked, it finally gave Sam and I a chance to talk about something other than the investigation. We chatted about our favorite moments from books, which movie adaptations we liked and which ones we didn't (she liked the Disney Chronicles of Narnia, but I forgave her for that), and what we hoped our favorite writers would do next.

"So," I said as we clambered over a massive boulder, "why

112

won't your parents let you have pets? You're so good with them."

Sam sighed, a big, long sigh even bigger and longer than she was.

"I guess I'll have to tell you at some point." She paused. But I waited. "I've always been big, even when I was younger. I'd try to play with the other kids, but I never fit in, sometimes literally. I couldn't fit on the swing set, I bent a slide so none of the other kids could use it, and when I was three I got stuck in a tube on the jungle gym."

Another pause.

"When I was five my parents bought me a hamster. I guess they thought I needed a friend since none of the other kids would talk to me anymore. I loved that little guy. I brought him everywhere with me, showed him all of my favorite spots in the woods and fed him all of my favorite treats. But one day when I was petting him, I guess I petted too hard. I killed him. I killed my first pet and my first friend."

There were tears in her eyes the size of pearls.

I patted her on the back, and tried to look into her eyes, but she kept looking away.

"It wasn't your fault," I said. "You were little. Well…you know what I mean. You were younger. Accidents happen. I once peed my pants at a birthday party when I was six. Accidents happen."

"Peeing your pants rarely kills things," she said.

"True, but that's not the point. If you did it on purpose, that would be something to be ashamed of, but you didn't. It was an accident, and you can't beat yourself up over that."

"Well my parents sure can," she said, the tears somehow getting even bigger without falling. "My dad called me a clumsy idiot, a giant waste of space, and told me I could never touch another animal again. Not ever." She sniffed. "I love animals, but

I'm always scared I'll hurt one again. That's why I never stuck up for you. I don't want to hurt anyone."

I nodded. "Look, I understand, okay? I really do. But….well I don't know what to say."

I looked down at Basset, which is what I usually do when I'm confused.

"Tell her I don't blame her. It might mean more coming from an animal. Besides, we're terrible at judging ourselves. We're either too hard or not hard enough. We can't see ourselves as clearly as others can. I see a girl who wants to take care of animals instead of hurting them. I see a girl who cares about others to the point that she doesn't even think about herself. And I see a girl who made one mistake a long time ago and should learn from it instead of running from it. We dogs have a saying: ignore the squirrels you can't catch, because barking at the squirrels in the trees will keep you from seeing the squirrels within reach. It means we shouldn't focus on the things we can't change. Instead, we should focus on the things we can. We can't change the past, but the future is ours."

"Squirrels, huh?" I said.

"Okay, so I made that saying up. But it's true. Focus on the squirrels on the ground because you can't reach the squirrels in the trees. The past is in the trees. The future is on the ground."

I told Sam everything Basset said, word for word.

"He really thinks all that?"

"He sure does. And I agree with him. You're so good with animals. I've seen it. You treat them like you really care. You can't let that one mistake define you."

She looked at me with a mix of hope and doubt.

"I don't know, but thanks anyway."

"Think about it," Basset said, looking directly at Sam instead of at me. "Trust me."

114

Sam got the message. She nodded.

We walked a bit further, past the "big rock."

"Your dad didn't take that very well, did he? He doesn't seem like the nicest guy."

Sam sighed again. "He's not. He tries his best, but he gets angry a lot." I gave her a worried look. "Oh, he never hits me or anything. Just with words. My mom barely even talks anymore because she doesn't want to get him riled up."

"So that's why you spend so much time out here."

"That's why."

I didn't have an answer for that one. A dad who's mean; is that a squirrel in a tree, or on the ground? Or somewhere in between? I had no idea how to deal with that, and I don't think Sam did either. And she's a lot smarter than I am.

"I'm sorry," I said. Even that little bit seemed to help.

"Thanks. Look, it's not a big deal. It could be worse. I just have to live with it. We all have things that don't go right. We just have to deal with them properly."

"You're right." I gave a little chuckle. "Take your own advice about that hamster."

Sam laughed out loud. "I will."

We finally made it to the end of the directions, and as we walked around the last boulder, the house came into view.

It was different than I had imagined.

It was even creepier.

Chapter 21
BASKERTONN MANOR

The manor was a massive Victorian-style mansion with a tall tower that sagged to the left like a wilting weed. All the windows were broken out, looking like empty eye sockets staring at you as you approached.

There were shadows in all the corners, and leaves choked all the doorways.

"It's real!" Sam said with an awed tone.

"Apparently."

"So if that part of the story's real..."

"Oh, I doubt the rest of the stories are true. I think it's *more* haunted than anyone says." I tried to laugh bravely, but it came out like a choked squeak.

Fine. I was scared.

I kept reminding myself that no one in their right mind would attack my personal giant Sam, but anyone running around robbing pet stores in a Halloween mask probably isn't in their right mind. And he could have friends.

There was also the problem of ghosts.

I don't believe in them. Not in my *head*. But my heart and my stomach sure seemed to believe in them.

"This is so cool!" Sam said. "Who knows what could be in

there?"

Yeah! Like spiders, rotting rats, and hidden bear traps!

I forced myself to get excited. After all, I *loved* exploring places like this. I was just getting worked up over some spooky stories. Like a kid.

"It's old enough there could be jewelry or some works of art that are worth serious money!" I said. "I bet there's all sorts of stuff in there!"

I pushed the fear down inside and acted excited. "Fake it 'til you make it," my mom always said.

We started to sneak towards the front door that gaped open like a hungry mouth, but the years and years of dead leaves made too much noise.

"Can't really creep up on this place," Sam said. "Besides, if anything's inside they'd have seen us by now."

I nodded, and we got up and strode straight for the house.

When we walked in the first thing I noticed was all the broken glass. It was littered everywhere, glittering like diamonds on the dirt-covered floor. Sharp, skin-ripping diamonds.

We'd have to be careful.

We were in a foyer about the size of my parents' entire house, with a wide staircase leading into darkness ahead of us. It was like those southern mansions you see in old movies like Gone With The Wind (don't laugh, my mom made me watch it): even now, covered in dirt and leaves and glass, you could tell it had been really fancy.

The carpet was deep red and looked extremely soft, and art *did* hang on the walls, but it wasn't anything that would be worth money. The pictures were ripped and tattered, the giant fancy frames chipping.

A chandelier about the size of my dining room table lay broken and shattered at the center of the entryway.

"Thank goodness that fell before we got here," Sam said.

"Yeah, but who knows what else is waiting to fall. We have to be careful."

Sam nodded, and Basset said, "I can scout ahead if you want. I'm less likely to get stuck anywhere and I can sniff out danger."

"If you think that's best, boy. But don't go out of eyesight. We should stick together."

I couldn't believe we were really *inside* the fabled Baskertonn Manor. Every single kid at school would be jealous if they knew Sam and I were the first ones in decades to explore it.

We carefully stepped around the chandelier, and, with Basset's nose leading us, we walked further in.

"Looks like there's a cellar door over there, and there's probably a dining room, kitchen, and some sitting rooms on this level," Sam said. "Bedrooms upstairs."

"Seems about right." I hesitated. "Let's save the basement for last."

"Good idea."

On this floor light filtered in through the broken windows, sending shafts of daylight onto the floor. There were shadows everywhere, but we could see well enough to walk without serious danger.

We made our way to the dining room, where another chandelier hung from the ceiling. It looked like the only thing holding it up was thousands of cobwebs as thick as a blanket.

There was more ruined artwork, but some of the paintings were in good enough shape that you could tell what they were.

"Looks like this is a portrait of some 'Indian shaman,'" Sam said. "I don't know if that's the right term, but that's what the plaque says."

"This one's just a bunch of horses," I responded, while

studying the painting. It was seven feet high and at least double that wide, and stretched from floor to ceiling. It was weird. Even in the gloom and even covered in dust you could tell the horses had way too many legs.

"Looks like the artist got a little distracted while painting the horses," I laughed. "Or didn't learn how to count."

I counted eight horses in all, and each one had twice as many legs as it should.

There were more paintings, but none of them were very interesting. There was a painting of an old man with wispy white hair who looked incredibly angry, but he almost made me laugh. His face looked like a little kid trying to look scary. He couldn't pull it off.

There was a painting of an old mansion called "Vale of Indescribable Indestructible Industry," and another painting of a Greek goddess.

"Looks like Athena," Sam said.

"Well someone actually paid attention in Mr. Grimley's history class," I laughed.

"I think I was the only one."

So far standard mansion stuff: paintings of old white men, castles, and Greek goddesses.

The table had eight chairs around it, and there were eight candelabras on the table, each one holding eight candles.

Again, nothing interesting. Interior decorators like to keep things consistent. At least that's what Mrs. Maplewood says.

We looked behind the paintings for hidden safes or secret doors, we looked under the table and under the rugs for trapdoors, but found nothing.

"I wish my dream had been more specific," I said. "Not a super helpful phantom."

Sam laughed. "I'm not an expert in phantoms, so maybe

that's how they all are."

We made our way into the kitchen. More dust, more cobwebs, more nothing.

The old stove was pretty cool: the size of a bus and loaded with old cooking tools that I had never seen. In an age when there wasn't electricity, everything looked so different.

It was all rusted, but there were hand mixers and some scales and other items that made me feel like I had stepped back in time.

It was in the next room that we found the first really interesting item.

We walked through a small door and into a much smaller dining room.

"Probably for eating breakfast," Sam said.

Again we looked at the paintings (another Athena, a few more Native Americans), and checked behind them, not really expecting to find anything.

But we did.

Chapter 22
HIDDEN PASSAGES

I pulled on the Athena painting, and with a bone-shaking creak it swung out on hidden hinges.

Behind it was a secret door.

"No way," I said breathlessly.

Sam came rushing over. "I thought secret doors were made up by mystery movies."

"Me too. I just figured there could be a safe or something."

I tried pushing the door, and it swung in easily.

An honest to God secret passage.

Behind the door was a small room, not much larger than a walk-in closet. The light from the windows barely made it into the room, but as my eyes adjusted to the dim light my heart sank a little.

This room was even more boring than the others.

The floor was littered with old newspapers and pages from books, all shriveled with age. There was no art on the walls, no furniture, nothing.

"I kinda got my hopes up I guess," I said.

"It's not a total bust. Now we know there are secret doors in this house. Who knows what else is out there?"

The only thing that was unusual was a framed needlepoint

that read:

"Follow the wrath

When the world takes a bath

And time removes its mask

Then you shall know thy task"

"Well that's weird," I said.

We made our way next to a small sitting room, with a grand piano that knelt down on only two legs. There were couches and chairs with a flowery pattern, and two huge leather chairs facing a small fireplace.

The mantle was made out of granite, and was intricately carved with all sorts of leaves and vines. At the top and center of the mantle was a carving of a human face, not much smaller than mine, with closed eyes and a peaceful, sleepy look on its face.

I remembered something from an old Frankenstein movie, and pushed on the face.

I guess there was no button to open up a secret compartment behind the fireplace.

Dang.

There were some old crystal decanters sitting on the side tables, all full of amber liquid.

"Those are probably worth something," I said, motioning to the crystal.

"Probably, but I'd feel bad taking anything from here. It's cool to explore, but I don't want to steal, even if it is from the dead."

I nodded. Exploring was fun, stealing was wrong.

But if there were some old baseball cards or something....well we'd cross that extremely unlikely bridge if we came to it.

My dad probably would have been excited by what was IN the crystal. Who knows how old and fancy the liquor was? Rare scotch? Thousand dollar brandy?

Personally, I had no interest. I don't like setting my throat on fire, as odd as that may be.

And old alcohol sitting in cobwebbed decanters for decades really didn't sound appetizing.

Sam and I moved on, the excitement from the secret door dulled somewhat by how little we'd found here.

Real life so rarely lives up to your daydreams.

We came to the last room on the first floor: a massive living room with a fireplace larger than my dad's car.

Everything in here looked expensive. Dusty, but expensive.

It looked like a scene from that Downton Abbey show. Once again, don't laugh; I once walked in on my mom watching it. I almost fell asleep at the sight of it.

More red leather chairs and couches, cracked like the ground in a desert. Another chandelier made entirely out of cobwebs. The smell of dust and age.

I felt like an archaeologist. This room in particular felt untouched. Undiscovered. Unexplored.

We walked around a bit, looking all over as much as we could.

Two of the walls were taken up entirely by gigantic, 20-foot tall bookcases. Now *this* got me excited. Leather-bound books from classic writers like Dickens and Goethe and tons of others that sounded boring, but old books fascinated me. They were like a doorway to the past, a way to share something with a person from 100 years ago.

Completely surrounding the fireplace, a massive tapestry covered the entire rest of the wall. It was the biggest work of art I had ever seen, fifty feet long and reaching all the way to the ornate ceiling.

In the fading light I could see it was an ocean scene, with

angry black waves pounding against two giants, who were standing on rocks rising out of the sea.

On the far left stood a man with a trident (Poseidon, I guessed), and on the right yet another depiction of Athena.

This didn't look like a friendly god-meeting.

Poseidon's trident was raised like he was about to throw it, and Athena's face looked like it was filled with hatred.

Why you would want two extremely peeved 20 foot tall Greek gods glowering down at you while you got comfortable with a good book I couldn't guess.

Not my idea of relaxing atmosphere.

Athena didn't have a weapon, but she was pointing a finger at Poseidon. My mom has proven that a nasty glare and a strong point can be just as frightening to a man as a trident. Maybe more frightening.

Someone had put a clock on the mantelpiece, though, right in front of Athena's pointing finger so it looked like she was extremely angry at the decorator's choice, instead of at Poseidon.

Sam and I each had the exact same idea at the exact same time: we both rushed over to the tapestry, lifted up an edge, and looked behind.

No hidden door.

We checked the other side. Still nothing.

I huffed a frustrated sigh.

"There *is* a hidden room, but there's nothing in it. There's a really strange tapestry, but it doesn't mean anything."

Sam nodded, plopping down in one of the leather chairs with a great puff of dust.

After she was done coughing, she looked around the room again.

"I can't figure it. This place seems like it has so many secrets to tell, but there's nothing here. Just dust and cobwebs and ruined furniture."

"Maybe upstairs?" I didn't sound hopeful.

"Yeah, maybe. But I doubt it. Maybe we're missing something."

We looked around the room again, but didn't notice anything.

"Maybe there's a clue in one of the books?" I asked.

"I like to read, but not *that* much," she laughed. "We couldn't work through those books in a year."

"I still feel like there's something hidden in here. It's the main room of the house."

Sam looked around again, her eyes settling on the tapestry.

She laughed. "Man, Athena sure hates that clock."

I looked up at the painting, and then it hit me.

The needlepoint poem.

"Sam! The clock!"

I ran over to it, and Sam watched me with a confused look.

"Follow the wrath when the world takes a bath! Athena's angrily pointing at the clock!"

I reached up, and fiddled with the glass over the clock face.

"And time removes its mask," I continued. "If I can take off its mask..." suddenly the glass swung outward with a little snap. I gently pulled on the clock hands, and the face of the clock came right off.

Behind it was a small, gold button.

Sam jumped up and rushed over to my side.

"Looks like I'm not the only one who can figure out a riddle," she said patting me on the back.

"Guess I was bound to be useful sooner or later."

I hesitated, but then went for it: I pushed the button.

Nothing.

We waited, listened.

Seconds ticked by, still nothing.

"Dang," I said. "I figured it out, but the stupid thing's broken."

"We might've hit a dead end," Sam said.

I didn't want to admit it, but it looked like we had.

The light outside was starting to fade, and I didn't really look forward to being in this big empty house in the middle of the woods in the dark.

"We should get going," I said, a defeated tone in my voice.

"Hey, maybe we'll have some ideas after we sleep on it." Sam was trying to remain optimistic. "Or maybe your phantom will come back."

"Oh, I'll look forward to it. My heart could use a bit more attacking."

Basset trotted ahead of us.

"Why don't you go and sniff around the outside of the house buddy?" I said. "See if there's anything unusual out there."

"Are you sure?" Basset looked worried.

"We've already searched this whole floor. There's nothing here that could hurt us. It's alright, you go ahead. We'll be fine."

Basset ran out of the room, stopping once to glance back at me.

We were almost through the smaller sitting room when I glanced over at the mantelpiece, and I jumped back and almost fell over one of the chairs. An icy pit had settled in my stomach.

The head on the mantelpiece.

It was looking right at me.

Chapter 23

THE SCREAMING FACE

My heart was pounding against my ribs as I steadied myself, blinked once, twice, and realized that it was real.

The face on the mantel was now awake.

The granite eyes had opened, and were now staring blankly out at the room. The eyes had no pupils, just solid gray, like the face of the dead.

"What is i– " Sam started to say, and then followed my gaze. "Ohmygosh."

She approached the face slowly. "Holy cow. How did that happen?"

I gathered myself and forced my voice to remain level. Didn't want a quiver of fear to escape.

"I don't know. It's not…. it's not like, alive is it?"

As soon as the words came out of my mouth I realized how ridiculous they sounded, but I couldn't take them back now.

Sam waved her hand in front of the eyes. No response.

"Of course not," I said. "I don't know why I said that. I meant 'it's not *moving*.' As in, it's not a machine, or a security system, right?"

"Not that I can tell," she said, leaning in for a closer look. "Jeez, that gave me a start."

"Not me. I just thought it would be fun to jump backward, trip over my own feet, and slam into a chair. You know. Got to liven things up somehow."

Sam laughed. "Of course."

"Stone face opening its eyes and glaring at us? Nothing surprising there."

I had regained my composure a little.

"Do you think it has something to do with the button I pushed?"

"Must." Sam was still studying the eyes. "I don't know why, though."

"You mean why would you hide a button in a clock that makes a statue's eyes open? Do you need a reason? Seems logical to me."

"Makes perfect sense."

I bent down next to her. I couldn't shake the feeling that those blank eyes were looking at me, staring right into my eyes and studying me. I shivered.

"Yeah, it's also creeping me out," Sam said.

"Distracting too." I reached up to cover the eyes with my hand so Sam and I could talk without the distraction. The second my hand closed over the eyes I felt a snap, and the statue's mouth gaped open.

Before I could even react, the head shrieked.

For the second time I jumped back and tripped. My heart decided to start dancing again.

A blast of steam was coming out of the statue's mouth, whistling like a teapot.

"What the-" Sam was cut off by an even louder snap. The head slowly started to sink into the mantel, and at the same time the rear of the fireplace started sliding back, with an awful dragging, grating sound.

128

"Another secret room!" Sam said in an awed whisper.

"Yeah, it's always a good idea to scare the pants off yourself whenever you go into a room. Personally, I like my doors to be pants-peeingly-terrifying too."

"I agree: it's weird. A weird way to hide a door."

Sam ducked into the fireplace, studying the head, which had now completely receded into the mantel.

"Compressed air or something," she said. "Like hydraulics. The air releases, the door opens. Clever."

"Good word. Shrieking hydraulic head. Clever."

Sam disappeared into the darkness, and with a deep breath to steady myself, I followed.

The room was tiny, about the same size as the last hidden room, but the walls were made of old quarried stone. Like the walls of a dungeon.

The room was lit in the flickering orange glow of two torches attached to the walls.

"Someone's been here," Sam said. "Recently."

I shivered again.

At the center of the room was a short stone slab, about the height of a table. In the center of the slab were a bunch of glass beakers and vials and tubes, all sitting in a pile of ash.

Pet carriers and cages were stacked up against the wall.

"It's like a laboratory," Sam said.

"Or an altar."

It was Sam's turn to shiver.

"What do you think was going on in here?" I asked.

"I don't know if I want to know." She sighed. "But I guess we have to find out. We need clues."

I looked at the pile of ash. It grossed me out, but Sam was right: we needed clues. I reached into the pile. I'd never stuck my hand in ashes before, and it wasn't quite what I expected: it was sandy but also somehow greasy. In the middle of the pile I felt something metal.

I pulled it out.

In my hand was a melted mess of something, a twisted pile of metal and glass that had fused together in a fire and re-hardened.

"What is it?" Sam asked, coming next to me for a closer look.

"I'm not sure," I said, but I had a good idea. The metal was silvery and thick. It looked like it had been a magnifying glass.

Like Guster's ant-burning magnifying glass.

"Look, we need to know what kind of ash that is, and what happened to the animals that were in these cages," Sam said. "You go out and find Basset. I'll follow right behind you with a sample of the ash and one of the cages."

She didn't need to tell me twice. I wanted out of that claustrophobic room.

I stepped out again, and was shocked by how dark it had gotten so quickly. There was just a tiny bit of gray light left, making every object in the room into a shadowy shape so you couldn't really tell what anything was.

"Better hurry up," I called back into the fireplace.

"You go ahead, I'll be right out."

I quickly made my way through the remaining rooms and out the front door.

Basset was nowhere in sight.

And that's when I heard the voices.

Chapter 24
GHOSTLY WHISPERS

I heard them the instant I came out the front door.

At first I thought it was just the rustling of the leaves in the wind, but soon I could pick out words.

Rising on the breeze, like silken strings fluttering in the twilight, I could hear the faintest voices. They sounded small, but definitely close, whispers rising and falling and rising again, whispers coming from the trees and the dark writhing leaves, harsh and cold. Each word sounded venomous.

Slowly, I could pick up more and more words until eventually I heard the same four lines repeated again and again.

"We are here and we are new

Ever we will rise on cue

Believe you we will rob

Something from all, the larges and the smalls."

Despite the lack of rhyming in the last two lines (so half the poem), and the vagueness of it, the poem did its job. The whispering voices all carried the same rhythm, chanting it away like a sullen prayer or a death march.

It was pretty creepy.

My mind was scrambling for a rational explanation. I scanned the shadows, the trees, everywhere, for signs of speakers or birds or *anything*, but there was nothing. The voices seemed to just come straight from the air.

I don't believe in ghosts.

I talk to animals, but that doesn't mean I believe every crazy cockamamie alien legend or the existence of fairies or ghosts.

I mean, do *you* believe in ghosts? So why should I, just because there's one weird thing about me?

Talking animals are real. Ghosts? That's ridiculous.

The whispered chants only lasted a couple of seconds, but it seemed like a lot longer to me.

I heard Sam coming towards the front door, and I turned around to ask her if she could hear the voices too. But the instant she stepped over the threshold and onto the forest floor, the voices cut short.

I decided not to bring it up. It was probably hard enough for her to believe in talking animals. Didn't want to give her any more evidence that I was a blathering nut job.

At that moment Basset came running around the side of the house.

"Nothing interesting to smell anywhere around here," he said with a disappointed tone. "Nothing to eat either."

"Not even some brown stuff?" I asked with a laugh.

Basset didn't look amused. He knows me too well.

"What's wrong?" he asked.

"Nothing," I didn't want to lie to him. "Look, I'll tell you later. It's probably nothing."

Sam and Basset gave me the same worried look, but didn't push it.

"Basset, we found another hidden room in there," Sam said. "I brought out a few clues and was hoping you could give them a sniff for us."

She set two of the animal cages down.

"I wondered what those were for," Basset said, eyeing them warily. "I got scared we were going on a surprise vet trip."

"We'd never trick you like that buddy," I said.

He went up to the cages and sniffed them. He went back and forth between them, sniffing again and again.

"What is it?"

"Nothing," he responded with a huff. "These were empty. No animals were ever in them."

"Weird," Sam said.

"Yeah, but at least we know that – whatever was going on in there – they weren't sacrificing puppies or something," I said.

"Was that a possibility?" Basset asked with a startled look.

"We also found this," Sam said, showing him a handful of the ash.

"Let me see," Basset said, giving it a couple of careful sniffs. He didn't want to inhale it. "Burnt paper and wood. That's it. Just a regular fire."

"Also weird," Sam said.

"So there's a hidden room with empty cages, and a small wood fire hidden behind a *fireplace*. Why not just use the fireplace instead of building a fire in a secret room behind it?"

"Maybe they were burning something they didn't want anyone to see. Evidence or something," Sam said.

"If it was evidence, it's destroyed. That ash is useless now."

"Yeah. I guess we should head back."

It was almost completely dark, but with Basset's nose leading us I was sure we'd be okay in the woods.

We made it back to civilization without any trouble, but I was jumpy the whole walk. Every rustle of leaves, every whisper of wind made me prick up my ears.

Those ghostly voices had me spooked.

During the walk we reviewed what we had learned.

Baskertonn Manor was real, and it was just as mysterious as we had expected. Based on the stolen cages, it was obvious the Masked Marauder was using the house as a base of operations.

But what were the cages for? What was he up to? And, most importantly, how could we stop him?

"We could stake out the place, you know, wait for him to arrive and catch him," Sam said. "Some of the stolen goods are there. That's evidence enough."

"I don't want you confronting any criminals face to face," Basset said. "Too dangerous. Why don't you call the police?"

"That's not a bad idea," I said. "The stolen cages *are* there, that's reason enough for them to go out to the house, and then *they* can do a stakeout."

"I guess," Sam said. "But a police interrogation won't think to ask him about the birds. We'll probably never find out what he was up to if the police get involved. And this was just a few burglaries; he'll be out of jail in a couple of years, and he can start his plan all over again."

I nodded. "True." I paused, thinking. "Look, my parents don't usually take the time to really pay attention to my problems and think them through, but they're smart. If I tell them I know where the Masked Marauder is hanging out, I think that'll get their attention. And they'll know what to do."

"Will you tell them about the birds?" Sam asked.

"I think so. They'll probably say it's nothing, but I'm more likely to convince my parents than I am to convince the cops. And the cops will definitely listen to my parents more than they'd ever listen to a kid."

"Good point. That sounds like a plan. Why don't you meet me out at the fort tonight around midnight if you can sneak out, and tell me how it went."

"Deal," I said as we approached my driveway. All the lights

were on, and I was sure dinner would be waiting inside. "See ya tonight!" I shouted as I waved.

"See ya!" Sam shouted back.

As we walked up the driveway I heard a familiar croak, followed by a high-pitched whistling. I looked down and saw a fat bullfrog sitting in the lawn like a blob of green Jell-O.

If green Jell-O was covered in warts.

Basset had introduced me to Gerald the bullfrog the first morning of summer vacation. Gerald was extremely friendly and lived in a small pond in the woods behind my parents' house.

"Where you boys been all day?" he asked in a raspy voice.

"Just exploring the woods," I said.

"Ugh," he responded, which sounded exactly like a froggy burp. "Wandering around all day. Just the thought makes me exhausted."

Frogs are notoriously lazy. The only thing fast about them is their tongues, and only when they're catching flies. They talk shockingly slowly.

"Speaking of, I ought to be getting back to the wife to get some sleep," he said, drawing out each word painfully. "If I get started now I should be home in four hours. Plenty of time."

His pond was about 300 yards away. I could carry him over there in two minutes.

I'd offered him a ride once or twice, but he always turned me down. He said my "breakneck speed" would make him sick, but I think he was really too proud to get carried around by a human.

"Alright, have a good night," I waved as he hopped once and stopped to catch his breath.

As we walked up the driveway, Basset's tail was wagging.

"Looking forward to some dinner, boy?"

"I sure am. But I'm also excited that this is almost over.

We've almost caught the bad guy, then we can go back to a normal summer."

"Yeah," I said with a sigh of relief. This had been exciting and kind of fun to piece together clues, but there was a lot of pressure. "It's almost over."

If only I knew: it was just beginning.

Chapter 25

KIDNAPPED

The second I walked into my house I knew there was trouble.

There was no noise. No Dad watching TV or Mom chatting on the phone with one of the village ladies. No microwave cooking up some dinner. Not even the clatter of dishes or the sound of footsteps.

Nothing.

"Mom! Dad!" I called out. The only sound was my own voice echoing back at me.

Maybe they had to stay late at work, or maybe the car had broken down. It wouldn't be the first time.

I raced over to the phone, but there were no messages from my parents. Just one from Mrs. Maplewood telling my mom that Mrs. Johnson's cream had gotten stolen again and she was in a fit over whatever neighborhood rascal had pilfered it.

That gave me a chuckle, but just a small one. I was too concerned.

What if they'd gotten in a bad car accident?

I calmed myself down and told myself they were probably just at a neighbor's having dinner. They would have left me a note on the fridge.

I turned around, and there was a note.

I breathed a huge sigh of relief.

I made my way over to the fridge, walking over something sticky on the floor. That was weird. My mom is usually pretty picky about keeping the house clean.

I stopped dead in my tracks.

"What's going on?" Basset asked, concern certainly filling his voice. "Where are your parents? You're white as a ghost."

The note on the fridge was written on a silk sheet the size of a napkin.

I went closer, and snatched it. It was covered in the same sticky stuff that was on the floor, but I barely paid any attention to that.

The note said: "We have your parents. Stop sticking your nose in other peoples' business or you'll find yourself an orphan. Don't tell the police. We have eyes everywhere. – The Masked Marauder"

My heart stopped and my hands got sweaty, making the note even stickier.

"What is it?" Basset asked. "I can't read."

I quickly shook the note off my hand and bent down and hugged Basset, a sob exploding out of my mouth.

"They took Mom and Dad," I burst out. "They took them and it's my fault. It's all my fault."

Basset leaned into my hug, as dogs love to do. "What do you mean they took them? They who?"

"The Masked Marauder and whoever he's working with. He left the note. They took Mom and Dad because I've been digging around."

I didn't want to cry. I was 13 for goodness' sake! But I couldn't help it. I was scared, but more than anything I felt guilty. This had been a fun game, figuring out clues and putting together the puzzle pieces, but it wasn't a game. My parents could get hurt.

"It's okay buddy, it's okay," Basset said soothingly while I was petting his back. "We'll find them. Once you've calmed down you can call the police and they'll solve everything."

"No!" I sobbed even harder. "The note said they'll kill Mom and Dad if I call the police!"

"They might just be saying that to scare you."

"Yeah, but they might not. I can't risk that. I . . . I just can't."

"I understand."

We were silent for a couple of minutes, a boy and his dog. There's no better comfort when you're sad, no better courage when you're scared, and no better friend when you feel alone.

"What do we do?" I asked.

"We find them." Basset sounded stern, tough, determined. "We find whoever took your parents and we bring them to justice. Together."

Chapter 26
MAKING A PLAN

Basset and I got up and went upstairs to my room.

I knew the Masked Marauder didn't want to hurt me. If he did, he would have waited at my house and grabbed *me* instead of my parents.

But I wanted to get out of there. I couldn't sleep in the house knowing the Marauder had been there. I felt like I was being watched.

I packed a suitcase full of necessities (toothbrush, change of clothes, flashlight, some granola bars and other snacks from the fridge, and of course a book) and raced back downstairs.

On my way out the door I glanced around the living room. I didn't know how long this would take. In fact, I didn't know if I'd *ever* be coming back here again. Who knew if I'd see Mom or Dad again? And if they did come home, would our lives ever be the same? Could we ever go back to "family time" and quiet dinners after my parents got kidnapped because of me?

I looked over at the ugly lamp on the table, and even that made me sad. The whole house just seemed so normal, like it was teasing me about how *not* normal my life was now. Even the lamp reminded me of my parents.

I looked over at a family picture we had taken just before

moving to Grant County, and I felt tears starting to well up in my eyes.

Before my stomach could twist itself into a knot I turned around, grabbed the door handle, and strode outside.

The night had gotten a lot colder, and thick clouds covered the moon so the only light was the sickly yellow of a streetlight way down the road.

Basset and I sprinted to the edge of the woods, and dove into the pitch darkness under the trees. I trusted Basset to lead the way, and kept my eyes on him as we ran. I had to trust him completely. He was the only thing I could see, a golden blur in a sea of black. A bottomless pit could have been two inches in front of me and I never would have known until I was plummeting down. So I kept my eyes on that golden blur and ran.

The cold was biting into my skin with sharp teeth. I hoped the fort was a little warmer.

I burst through the oak door and found the fort lit with an inviting orange glow and filled with cozy warmth.

Sam was tending a fire that crackled in the stove, and she had lit candles all over the room for some light.

"You're early," she said casually, not turning from the fire. "Probably a good thing though. If you came at midnight like we had planned you would've frozen. It's getting cold out there."

"What are you doing here already?"

"My old man came home in a mood, and then left right away to head down to the bar with some buddies. He won't get home until late, and when he does he won't notice I'm gone. Figured there was no reason for me to wait to come down here."

"Okay," I said, not sure what else to say. How do you bring up the fact that your parents have been kidnapped? It's not a conversation you cover when you're learning about good manners.

Sam turned from the fire to say something, and she

stopped dead in her tracks.

"What is it? What's happened?"

"My parents are gone." I tried to sound brave, but I ended up sounding kind of angry.

"What do you mean gone? You mean like, out at a restaurant or something?"

I shook my head. I was shocked at how I felt when I said it out loud. I didn't feel scared or alone. I felt livid. Someone had stolen my parents, and I had to get them back.

"No. I mean that monster the Masked Marauder took them."

Sam jumped up. "My gosh. This . . . this is serious. But I'm with you. We'll get them back." She looked over at Basset. "The three of us."

I nodded, the anger simmering inside me.

"What do we do?" Sam asked. "Want to call the police?"

I explained everything to her, about the note and the warning on it.

"I agree with both of you," Sam said looking from me to Basset and then back to me. "The Marauder is probably bluffing. It's extremely unlikely he'll know if we call the police. But it's too risky to tell the cops, or to talk to anyone else really. The safety of your parents, the birds, this village, and maybe even the entire world is up to us."

"No pressure."

"Yeah. None. Piece of cake."

"Easy as pie."

"You're both making me hungry," Basset said. He looked kind of embarrassed at having said that.

"I know, me too," I said. "Neither of us have had dinner."

"Me neither," Sam said. "Not much in the fridge, but I have a few things lying around this place."

"I feel bad stopping to eat with my parents out there."

"Look, we have to know where they are before we can get them. We have to be very careful about this and think it through. And I don't know about you, but I don't think very well when I'm hungry."

That was true.

I pulled out my granola bars and some hot dogs, holding out a hot dog for Basset, which he quickly gobbled up.

Sam opened a cupboard made from old house shutters and pulled out some graham crackers, marshmallows, and chocolate.

"It'll be like camping out," she said. "We'll make s'mores and hot dogs over the fire and we'll stay up all night if we have to to figure this out."

I liked the sound of that. I'd always wanted to do a campout like this. I just wished my first campout didn't have to be because my parents had gotten kidnapped. I don't think "how do we rescue my parents from a madman" is the standard campout conversation.

We put our food on some sticks and held them over the fire. We soon had quite a feast for ourselves.

"We have a lot of clues," Sam said while we ate. "A lot. We just need to use them."

"I know," I said. "I feel like we have all the puzzle pieces, we just have to figure out how they all fit together."

I felt frustrated. We really had done a lot of investigating, but everything seemed so scattered, so hazy.

We knew what the Masked Marauder had stolen (Indian artifacts, hardware, pet supplies, comic books). We knew where he was hiding out (Baskertonn Manor). We had the ID card with a few readable letters, and we had a melted hunk of glass and metal. Lastly we had the clues from the masked phantom at my window: a rhyming riddle and some numbers.

"You don't think the masked man at my window is the Masked Marauder, do you?"

"That seemed like the obvious answer at first," Sam said. "But why would he give you clues to catch himself?"

"Unless he's trying to throw us off the trail?"

"I don't think so. There's easier ways to do that than repelling off someone's roof and giving them cryptic riddles."

"Yeah," I said.

We talked a bit more about each of the clues, trying to fit them together.

"When the indoor sun is upside down
And the smile becomes a frown
Then the answers will appear
Never known to be so near."

"Upside down sun could mean 'nighttime,'" I said. "And that part about a smile becoming a frown could be talking about tonight. I mean, I was excited when I got home, and now at night I'm really upset."

"Yeah, but the next part is 'Then the answers will appear.' I don't see any answers around here."

After a lot more conversations like that – coming up with ideas that ended up not really making sense – I asked if we should just try a stakeout at Baskertonn Manor after all.

"We might have to," Sam said. "If we can't think of anything else. That might be where your parents are."

"That's far too dangerous," Basset said from where he was lying beside me in front of the fire. "We don't know if that's where they are. It could be a trap, and I don't want you wandering into something unprepared."

"Yeah, but what else can we do?" I asked.

"If there's too much traffic on a highway you want to cross, you don't just rush out there anyway," he said. "That's a good way to get hit by a truck. You wait until everything's right."

"That's true, I guess."

Eventually, when we had hit yet another dead end, I decided the time was right to tell them my Guster Liberman theory.

"Look, I know it sounds like I'm just trying to get revenge on him because he's so mean to me," I said after telling them my evidence. "I know I'm biased. But I think it makes sense."

"You're right," Sam said. "All the pieces fit together perfectly. The letters are right on the ID, the glass and metal could be a melted magnifying glass, and he sure hates birds. If anyone at school could be a criminal, it would be him."

"I'd love it if it was him," Basset said. "I want him out of your life as much as you do. And we could take him, the three of us. But do you think he's smart enough to do all this? To figure out how to chase the birds away and kidnap your parents?"

"I know," Sam said. "He's either a secret genius, or he's not doing this alone."

"If Guster's a secret genius we might as well start believing a band of flying pigs will come and rescue my parents. It's just as likely."

"Then he's not working alone," Basset said. "And that makes him dangerous."

"Even worse, it means we don't know who or what or how many we're up against," Sam said.

I gave a very frustrated sigh and turned to look into the fire.

"Okay, let's go over the riddle again," Sam said.

"Oh my gosh! How many times can we go over it?" I shouted. "We're not going to figure it out! We're getting nowhere!"

I threw the rest of my hotdog into the fire, sending sparks flying.

Basset started licking my hand, and I jerked away. I didn't *want* to be comforted right now.

"Sit down, Nate," Basset said forcefully. "Sit!"

I sat. He'd never told me what to do before.

"I know you're angry. I know you're scared. I know you're frustrated. I've been all of those things myself. But you can't let your emotions control you or get the better of you. You just can't. You're a human. You're better than that. You can ignore your emotions and choose how you act. And right now, you need to choose to act calm. You need to choose to think this through, or your parents are goners."

"Look," Sam said cautiously. "I get mad at my old man. A lot. But I don't let that control me. I choose to be nice to him because that makes our lives a lot easier. When I get frustrated, I just act calm. I fake it until I make it. I can't control how I feel, but I can control how I act, you know?"

I felt embarrassed. Like when I got so frustrated that I threw a video game controller at the floor and broke it. Over a game.

This was no game. But I still felt foolish for throwing a temper tantrum.

"Sorry," I said. "Let's go over that riddle again."

"It's okay," Sam said, looking at Basset. "We both understand. Believe me. Basset probably understands frustration better than anyone. It's hard, but we have to do this together."

I tried to think, but it was hard. I was tired, and all those other emotions were still blurring my thoughts.

"I know I said we could stay up all night," Sam said. "But I'm starting to think we need to try and sleep. We need to get a fresh start in the morning."

I agreed. I felt guilty sleeping while my parents were trapped somewhere waiting for my help, but I didn't think I could help them with my eyelids as heavy as lead.

Sam went over to another cupboard (this one made from an old wooden icebox) and pulled out two sleeping bags. They were really old and ratty, but they were clean and extremely warm. Sam and I rolled them out next to the fire, and we settled down with Basset curled up between us.

"Try to sleep, buddy," Basset said. "I know you don't want to, but you need to rest."

"I know," I said. I really didn't think I'd be able to. I was so worried about my parents and feeling guilty and scared.

"I'll keep watch over you tonight," Basset said. "You know I'm a light sleeper, and if anything makes so much as a whisper outside I'll jump right up and investigate."

"Thanks boy. I know you'll look out for me." I scratched him behind the ears and he smiled.

I settled my head down, and watched as the fire burned lower. To my surprise, I fell almost instantly asleep, with the image of the embers playing in my eyes and the words of the riddle echoing in my ears.

Chapter 27

THE UPSIDE DOWN SUN

I awoke with a start around dawn, after a nightmare about my parents caught in a giant spider's web. It was a perfect metaphor for how I felt: trapped in a web.

The embers of the fire were still burning a deep orange color, and Sam and Basset were still asleep.

I felt rested, but stiff and a little groggy. I knew I'd never be able to get back to sleep after that dream, but I didn't want to wake up my friends until they were ready.

I sat watching the light in the embers ebb and glow while the words from the riddle still swam around my brain.

As I slept, the last line of the riddle had been especially loud in my head. "Never known to be so near. Never known to be so near."

We hadn't really gone over that part much. It didn't seem as important as the rest of the riddle. After all, the first two lines told us how to *get* the answers, the last line was after we had already found the answers.

But now it seemed important. I figured it was probably because my unconscious brain had been focusing on it, but I couldn't shake the nagging feeling I was missing something right in front of my face, just like how I had missed the riddle itself on the window at first.

The meaning was obvious now that I really thought about it. The answer is near. That must mean somewhere close by, maybe even in my house.

While I watched the light of the fire, I started running over things in my house that could hold clues: my mom's china cabinet, under my bed, in the basement. The most obvious place was behind the crawlspace door, but there was no way to get in there.

It was funny. The light from the fire was almost the exact same color orange as that ugly lamp my dad loved so much.

"The lamp!" I shouted, making Basset and Sam both jump to their feet in an instant.

Basset barked loudly, and then realized there was no intruder, just me.

Sam looked groggily at me.

"What'd you say? A ramp? Where?"

"No! The lamp! My parents' old lamp!"

"The ugly one you said your dad found in the basement? What about it?"

Basset was looking at me like I might be sleepwalking. And sleeptalking.

"Think about it! It's big and round and a unique color orange. Like…"

I trailed off, seeing if they could figure it out themselves from there.

It was too early in the morning.

They were tired.

"Like an egg," Basset said. "I like eggs. I could go for some eggs right now."

"Orange juice?" Sam asked.

Hungry too, I guess.

"The sun." I said finally. "Like the sun. Indoors."

Sam slapped her forehead. That woke her up.

"An indoor sun. An electric lamp." She rolled her eyes. "It really is the obvious things that you miss, the things right in front of your face."

"I know," I said. "But riddles always look more obvious once you've solved them."

Basset wasn't so easily comforted. He was a little bitter about it. "Who calls a lamp an indoor sun? That's stupid. Even animals know how electricity works. Okay, we don't know *how* it works, but we know what it is. Only *wild* animals don't know that."

I laughed. "That's just how a riddle works I guess buddy. C'mon, let's take a look at that lamp."

We sprinted out the door, but not before making sure we grabbed our supplies and a couple of granola bars on the way. Growing kids need their breakfast. Especially six foot tall ones.

The excitement had returned. We were back on the trail, back on the hunt. We could do this.

We made it to my house in no time, and we ran right up to the dining room table.

"I'm with your mom on this one," Sam said. "Ugliest freaking lamp ever."

"Definitely," I said, grasping it by the neck and flipping it over.

On the base, right above the center, were two holes about the size of my fingers. Below that was a thin, curved crack.

Like a face. Two eyes and a smile.

I put my fingers in the holes and gave the base a half turn so the smile was upside down.

With a click, the bottom panel popped off.

Inside the base was a tiny hidden compartment, and in the compartment was a key.

An old, rusty key with no note or any markings. But I knew

what it went to.

"C'mon," I said, snatching the key and setting the lamp down carefully (I didn't want to have to explain a broken lamp after I'd rescued my parents, even if it did make my mom happy).

Sam and Basset exchanged a confused look, but followed me as I bounded up the stairs.

I stopped at the crawlspace door, knelt down, and slid the key into the top lock.

Perfect fit.

"What's in there you think?" Sam asked as I removed the first lock.

"I have no idea," I said as the second one came free. "But if the riddle is right, it's answers."

"Do you think it's safe?" Sam asked just as I slid the key into the last lock.

I hesitated. Basset crawled right in front of me and did a quick sniff-check.

"All clear," he said. "No animals, no unusual chemicals, nothing. Go for it."

I undid the last lock, and the crawlspace door swung open.

Chapter 28

INSIDE THE CRAWLSPACE

Inside was a small room – much more than a crawlspace – with a ceiling high enough that I could stand up without bumping my head.

The floor was covered in a thick coat of dust that hadn't been disturbed in a long time. No animal prints or footprints disturbed the surface.

The room looked ordinary enough: old musty boxes were stacked up all over the place, turning the attic into a maze.

All of a sudden we heard that fast ticking again, for just a second or two, and then silence.

"What the heck was that?" Sam asked.

"I don't know, but I've heard it before. Always from in here."

We cautiously made our way into the first corridor between the boxes, with Basset's nose leading the way.

Sam and I switched on our flashlights and swept the aisle. There were a lot of shadowy side passages that could be hiding anything.

Or anyone.

It made me nervous, but I kept reminding myself that the dust had been undisturbed.

That only helped a little.

In the center of the aisle we found an old tattered book, lying open.

I stooped down and picked it up, reading the cover.

"A children's grammar primer," it said.

It was open to a page about the alphabet, with a numbered list of all the letters:

1.	A
2.	B
3.	C
4.	D
5.	E
6.	F
7.	G
8.	H
9.	I
10.	J
11.	K
12.	L
13.	M
14.	N
15.	O
16.	P
17.	Q
18.	R
19.	S
20.	T
21.	U
22.	V
23.	W
24.	X

25.   Y
26.   Z

All the other pages had simple poems to help kids learn to read.

Everything else up here was in boxes. It seemed odd that this book had been left out.

I scanned the boxes, and saw that my mom had been right: a lot of them were labeled "Christmas" and one even said "Aluminum Christmas Tree." Might as well have said "tacky" right on it.

A few of the boxes had fallen over, spilling their contents out onto the ground: mostly books or old plates and silverware, but there were a few baseball cards. I'd definitely have to come back up here. You know, once my parents weren't in mortal danger.

The ticking came back, just for a second.

"It sounds like it's coming from over there," I said, motioning to one of the side passages on the right.

We snuck our way over and turned the corner.

I finally saw what had been making all that ticking this whole time.

And I wished I hadn't.

Spiders.

Thousands and thousands of scurrying spiders.

Chapter 29
THOSE WHO AWAKENED

I gasped and jumped back, bumping into Sam and bouncing right off her. I tripped and fell face down on the ground.

There was that ticking, scurrying sound again, right in front of me. I looked up; a sea of spiders rushing at my face. Just as the spiders reached me I scrambled onto my hands and knees.

I tensed up, expecting to feel hundreds of tiny, venomous fangs sink into my skin.

Instead, the spiders rushed around me, like waves breaking around a rock, and then they stopped, all their beady eyes looking up at me.

I was pretty sure I could crawl over them and squish most of them on my way to safety, but I'd definitely get bitten a bunch of times. And who knew how venomous these things were? They were awfully big and hairy.

Sam and Basset both stood back, outside the circle of spiders, probably too cautious to move out of fear that the spiders would leap at me.

Through the crowd, I saw a much larger spider approaching me. All the critters were gray, but this one looked almost stark white, with black splotches on its back. The sea of spiders parted as he walked through, all eight of his eyes staring

155

right at me.

It was a somber, terrifying mood, which was almost instantly broken.

"Sheesh, you *finally* made it in here," the big spider said. "We've been waiting long enough. This is important, you know. Not just a social call."

"You can *talk*!" I shouted. Sam looked surprised, and Basset looked positively dumbfounded.

"Well *someone's* observant," the spider continued. "Really, spot on investigation there kid. Next thing you know, you'll be able to figure out that I have eight legs!"

I just stared.

"But, I thought bugs and little things couldn't talk."

"You thought wrong." Then the spider laughed. Yes, laughed, and it was a surprisingly friendly laugh. Not sinister and "I'm going to eat you"-toned at all. "I'm just messing with ya. C'mon back to our nest and I'll explain everything."

The spider turned around and walked the way he had come, and all the other spiders followed, quickly disappearing into the darkness.

"What the vet?" Basset said under his breath. I'd never heard him swear before.

"What's going on?" Sam asked.

"I don't know," I responded. "Spiders can apparently talk now. Weird week."

"Ooooooookay."

"And they want us to go back to their nest so they can explain everything to us."

"Ummmm…."

Sam wasn't usually speechless.

She shook her head to clear it. "Do we trust them?"

"Not a chance," Basset said.

"I'm not so sure," I responded. "They could've bitten me a hundred times before I'd had the chance to blink. And he seems friendly enough."

"Friendly? Really?" Sam asked.

"Yeah. More Charlotte's Web than The Hobbit, I guess."

"Well let's see what they want," Sam said, taking this easier than I would have thought.

She rolled with the punches a lot better than I did.

Basset looked at me cautiously.

"You keep your eyes to the rear and make sure they don't surround us. We can make a quick escape at the first sign of trouble. Okay boy?"

"Okay," he said, clearly still not convinced.

We made our way deeper into the shadows, making sure to watch our step for any stragglers. You don't want to get off on the wrong foot, if you know what I mean; crushing someone's family isn't the best way to get a new friendship started.

Our flashlights found the nest, and I gasped out loud.

The webs glittered in the light like diamonds, stretching from floor to ceiling across the corridor, about five feet wide. The cobwebs receded backwards, layer after layer after layer, hundreds of thousands of tiny strands building a deep, almost impenetrable cloud.

It wasn't a nest. It was a spider city.

The lead spider – I don't know what they call them, spider kings maybe? – was waiting for us at eye level on a bridge of glistening web. He was surrounded by about 30 of his little friends, all staring me in the eye.

"Good of you to join us," he said.

"Ummm… thanks for the invite." I was trying to be polite, but I wasn't an expert in spider etiquette. "My name's Nate."

"Yes, we are aware. We live in the same house, you know."

"Oh, right," was all I could muster.

"I'm William Webwood the 1,134th," he said. "I'd bow, but we have no knees, you see. Or waists."

"Of course," I said, bowing myself.

"Look, I'm sure you have many questions, the lot of you. Let me start off with the most obvious: yes, we can talk. And no, we have not been keeping this a secret from you. It only started about a month ago. For generations we were little more than savage beasts, bugs scurrying to and fro with no awareness of ourselves. But then, suddenly, that all changed. It was like waking from a deep sleep, but also not like that at all. Imagine being born as an adult. One minute you're not there, and the next minute you are."

"Sounds like that'd take a bit of getting used to."

"Oh believe me, it did. We'd never had consciousness, you know. Quite disconcerting. But we were not the only ones."

"There's more?" Basset asked. "How many? All the bugs?"

"We do not know how many of our brothers have awakened, but we know that we are not the only. And we are not the first. There is a darkness brooding out in the wider world, a darkness that we have sensed as much as seen, whispers floating in the air bringing news of destruction."

"Sounds serious," I said.

"Oh, quite. Believe me, we prefer not to be so glum and somber. But it's the only way to talk about such things."

I nodded. "Got it."

"We heard news of your gift, of your ability to hear us. That is why we called you up here."

"Wait, called me? What do you mean?"

"From your window. Remember? Floating face appearing in the night? Is that a common occurrence among humans?"

"That was you?"

"Who else would it have been? You know a lot of flying phantoms?"

"Well no. But how?"

"We're quite clever," he said. If he'd had a nose, I'm sure he would have pointed it up in pride. "We knew you'd be terrified of a few thousand spiders waking you up, so we built a puppet. You know, something you'd be a little more comfortable with."

"Comfortable! That thing was terrifying! Why was it wearing a mask?"

"Yeah, turns out we're not very good at making realistic human faces out of webs," he sounded offended. "We were only born a couple days ago. Give us a little slack, would ya? You try making a realistic human face out of yarn you spit out of your butt and tell us how it goes. We'll wait."

"Sorry."

"Obviously our puppet couldn't speak, which is why we wrote our message on your window."

"It was kind of cryptic. I know, I know, you were just born and all that. But why the vague poetry?"

"You found our school book in the corridor, correct? That is how we learned to spell. At the start, that was all we had to go on. If poems are how you teach your children how to read, we figured that was how you all talked. We assumed you were a very rhymey civilization."

"Okay," I said. I was trying to process all of this. It made a surprising amount of sense, but it really wasn't what I expected. I was having a little trouble asking questions while I was still processing the answers. "So you left us clues telling us where to search. How did you know about Baskertonn Manor?"

"Whispers on the breeze my friend, whispers on the breeze. We don't know all the details, just bits and pieces. What we know is that darkness is coming, and you are our best hope for stopping it. So we passed along whatever we heard to you."

I passed along all this info to Sam, who, as usual, took it easily.

"That makes sense," she said, when I was done.

"That's news to me."

"Well, it's not a normal kind of sense, but it makes its own sense."

I turned back to the spiders.

"So do you know where my parents are? Who took them?"

"We do not. Not everything. But we called you up here to promise you our help. We have always been peaceful spiders, even if the previous owner tried to hide us away in here."

"The previous owner knew about your nest, that's why he sealed up that door so tight? Why didn't he just call an exterminator?"

"Wow, thanks. 'Why didn't he just wipe out your entire family?' You say it so casually."

"I'm sorry. I just mean, from his perspective."

"He found us just days before your parents bought the house. He didn't want to spend the money on an exterminator, but didn't want your parents to back out of the deal because of a few thousand spiders."

"So he shut this place up tight until the sale was final," I nodded. "Sneaky."

"Very."

"So you're offering your help," Basset said from behind me. "I'm cautious around your kind, mostly because we haven't had much of a chance to get to know you, but we're happy for any help we can get. How do you propose to help us?"

"Thank you Basset," William said. "We've heard that you are a reasonable, patient, and wise animal. Seems your reputation was correct." Basset got that blushing look on his face again.

"First, we can be your eyes and ears out in the wild. Without birds to peck us off, we can travel safely and swiftly all over. And we're more trustworthy than those nasty squirrels."

"I'm starting to like them," Basset whispered to me.

"Second, we heard you and Basset talking about needing to read something that will provide the name of our enemy. We heard the name back in our infancy, and tried to communicate it to you, but we were unsuccessful. And now the name has been lost. I do not know how our message failed, but I am looking into it."

"Thank you," I said. "How can you help us read the card?"

"Tell me, have you ever heard of the ogre faced spider?"

I shuddered at the name.

"Oh yes, they are quite terrifying," William said, noticing my reaction. "Deadly hunters who can jump on you from quite a distance before you've even noticed them. They also throw their webs like a lasso. A sticky, sticky lasso. Luckily, they don't live this far north."

"Then why do you mention it?" Basset asked.

"Because if anyone can help you read that card, it is an ogre faced spider. Their eyesight is legendary."

"Doesn't do us a lot of good if we have to go to Mexico to find one," Basset said.

"There is one near here. Somewhere deep in the woods. Legend has it that he cast his web over a bird and rode it 3,000 miles here for a change of scenery."

"That's insane," I said.

"Of course it is. He was probably brought here as a pet and released when his owner got bored of him. But the legend is so much more interesting."

"I thought you said you were more trustworthy than squirrels," Basset growled.

"I told you the truth. Just an interesting anecdote first.

Anyway, if we can find him, he can certainly see the letters on your card. Assuming of course that he became conscious when we did. And assuming that he can read."

"We might have to teach a spider to read," I relayed to Sam.

"Well that sounds interesting."

"What are we waiting for?" I asked. "Let's find ourselves a terrifying spider and see if it will help us read an ID card."

Chapter 30

SEARCHING FOR AN OGRE

It was decided that the spiders would spread out over the entire forest and find their ogre-faced cousin while the rest of us waited at the fort.

They figured spiders would draw a lot less attention than three "giants stomping through the leaves like elephants." That's how they said it at least.

This was especially important since our enemy knew that I was on to him, and my parents were in danger if I was spotted poking around. I had to stay out of it until the last second.

The spiders tried to be sympathetic, but they weren't very good at it.

"I'm terribly sorry for your loss," one of them – who introduced himself as Frank – said to me. "I know it must be troubling for you. Well, I mean, I don't know from experience. My father was crushed by a basketball and my mother was sucked up into a vacuum when I was still in my egg sack, but I didn't really mind. It was back when we weren't truly awake yet. It's hard to care when you don't have thoughts to care *with*."

"It's also hard to care when your parents don't pay much attention to you," another interjected. "Not their fault. My mom had 2,132 babies. Hard to keep tabs on all of them, even with eight legs and eight eyes."

"True," Frank said. "Still, it must be hard for you. I guess. Come to think of it, I'm actually not sure what my parents' names *were*. Bertha and Sean? Santana? Shroom? Is that even a name?" He wandered off, quite distractedly muttering to himself as he went. "Smiley? No. Why would a spider be named Smiley?"

It cheered me up, but not for the reason they hoped. They made me laugh.

Sam and Basset and I returned to the fort, with a handful of spiders to "keep guard." I wasn't sure how much good a half-inch spider would be in a fight, but I was glad for the company.

"Once we're done defeating the darkness, what do you think we'll do?" one of them asked while we walked.

"Do? What do you mean? We'll go back to eating and building webs I guess."

"But, I mean, you don't think we'll go back to sleep, do you? I like being able to think and being able to talk. I'll miss it."

"How can you miss it if you aren't smart enough to remember it?"

"I don't know. But I think I will."

"Me too," another said. "And is that all we'll do? Just eat and build?"

"That's all we've ever done before."

"Human, what do you do? When you're not fighting mysterious dark forces, I mean? What's the meaning of your life?"

I opened my eyes wide as saucers and looked at Sam.

"That might be the most important question each person has to ask," Sam said, like she had thought of this already. I sure hadn't. "We all have to figure out what we're best at, what we like to do, what we're here for. Then we have to use our skills to help others and make the world a better place. Some people say God put us here to learn that: how to help, how to care. Not everyone figures it out, mind you. Not everyone even thinks to ask, actually. But that's one of the fun parts about being alive: figuring things out."

"Oh," the first spider said. "Sounds hard."

I laughed. "You'll get used to it."

"Assuming we don't forget everything and turn back into mindless beasts."

"Yes, assuming that," I said.

We got back to the fort in short order, and Sam built the fire back up. It wasn't particularly cold, but it gave her something to do. I just sat and thought. A dangerous thing to do when you're worried.

What was happening to my parents right now? Were they getting tortured for information? Were they locked in some kind of dungeon?

Basset could always read me.

"They'll be okay buddy. Trust me. We'll get them. We have allies now."

"Thanks boy," I said, scratching him behind his ears.

Sam could read both of us.

"We've come a long way from this morning," she said. "This morning all we had were puzzle pieces. Now we've put a lot of them together, and we have help for the rest."

While we made ourselves a hotdog lunch we talked over the remaining clues.

It really was encouraging that we had figured out the phantom at the window. We had unraveled the riddles and come to the solution.

That gave me a lot of hope.

We talked about the glass and metal again, theorizing about what else it could be if it wasn't a magnifying glass. We didn't come up with a lot of alternatives.

Sam wondered if all the Athena paintings meant anything, but I said the owners of the manor were probably just trying to class the place up with some classical art. It worked a lot better than my dad's grandma-lamp, though I had to admit I was glad he kept it. We would've been lost without that key.

"Look, I know you guys said you thought we talked in rhymes, but why did you call the lamp an upside down sun?" I asked the spiders.

"You try learning all the words for everything in the world in a week," one of them said. "I think we did pretty well."

I laughed. "Sorry. No, you did great. We figured it out in the end."

Sam had a look on her face like she was starting to figure something else out.

"You guys have no idea who this 'darkness' is, right?" she asked the spiders.

"None," one of them said.

"We just heard bits and pieces, mostly from birds perched on the roof or on the telephone wire outside. Once they disappeared we knew it was getting serious."

I told that to Sam, who nodded.

"Tell me, are there evil spiders out there?"

"Why do you ask that?" I asked.

"Just curious."

"I don't know," one of them said like he'd never thought of it before. "I honestly don't even know if there are other spiders out there who've awakened."

"I think William said there are," I said.

"Well there you have it."

"But evil ones?"

"Maybe. I have no way of knowing. Are there bad humans?"

"Oh yes. Lots I suppose. More good ones though. And there's a lot of people caught somewhere in between."

The spider sounded thoughtful. "Well then I suspect it's the same for spiders. Some good, some bad, and a lot in between."

"We're the good ones though, right?" another asked

"I think so," the first said slowly. "I hope so. I don't want to be evil. But how can you tell?"

"By choosing not to be," Sam said with a laugh when I relayed the question to her. "If you don't want to be evil, then don't be. It's easy enough to tell the difference."

"How?"

"Just listen to your heart," I offered. It was terrible advice from lazy movies, but it was the only thing I could think of.

"Mine just says 'thump,'" one said. "That's not very helpful."

"We use our hearts to help us walk," another said. "Our legs fill up with blood like blood-balloons. How does that tell us what's right and wrong?"

"Oh boy," I said.

"I'll explain it to you later," Sam laughed. "But part of it is choosing not to be selfish. You can feel selfish, but you have to choose not to give in to it and choose to help others, even when it doesn't help you. You've already got that covered."

We talked for hours like this, revisiting the clues occasionally but mostly chatting with the spiders. They were curious about so many things that their questions were practically endless.

It was honestly kind of fun getting to know them and talking to someone who had such a unique, fresh perspective on everything. They didn't even know what part of the world they were in. Though I suppose spiders don't have to worry about geography too much.

Just as long as there's plenty of flies where they are.

And flies are everywhere.

Time flew by as we talked, which was merciful, since my worry was tying knots tighter and tighter in my stomach.

Before I even knew it, it was late in the evening, and Sam recommended we get some rest.

Spider messengers came once or twice to update us. There really wasn't any news.

Like the night before, I was positive I wouldn't get any sleep but I was out of it as soon as my head hit the pillow.

Worry takes its toll on you.

I had more dreams about my parents. This time they were trapped on a rock in the middle of the ocean, with Athena glaring at them from another rock, and Guster dressed in a toga and no shirt (an image I hope to never see again as long as I live, by the way) chucking tridents at them.

Dreams are confusing.

At some point in the dead of night I felt something tickling my arm. It woke me up slowly, but I figured it was just Basset's tail brushing up against me.

Until I felt the tickle move onto my shirt, up my neck, over my lips and onto my nose.

Then my eyes snapped open and I screamed.

Eight pitch-black eyes were staring at me.

I sat bolt upright, and the spider on my nose slipped and fell onto my cheek, letting out a scream of his own, but he quickly scrambled back onto my nose.

"Goodness, you can kill a spider jerking around like that," he said while I struggled to focus on him. "You're lucky my instincts didn't kick in. We pack quite a bite."

It was William. He had returned.

Sam and Basset were awake and alert now, both staring

with wide eyes at the spider on my face.

"I don't usually wake up to arachnids gazing into my eyes," I said. "It's a bit startling."

"I suppose it could be," he said in an offhand way, like he was shrugging. That would be ridiculous of course: spiders don't have shoulders. "Anyway, I bring news."

I kept silent, holding my breath. Did he find my parents? Were they dead?

"We found him. The ogre-face. He has asked to meet with you."

Chapter 31
MEETING AFTER MIDNIGHT

It was still a few hours before dawn and the air was so cold it was like it was sucking all the warmth out of me. I could barely even remember what it felt like to be warm.

I kept following the spiders through the forest. I had to. If I was ever going to see my parents again and make this right, I had to.

Basset trotted along somberly at my side, and Sam was next to him.

"You can go back," I said to Sam through chattering teeth. "It's cold out here, and who knows what's waiting for us out there in the dark? You don't have to be here."

"Yes I do," she said simply. "I'm not going anywhere."

"Me neither," Basset said.

I couldn't convince them. If anything happened to either of them I knew I'd never be able to forgive myself, even if they did decide to come on their own. They were still out here because of me.

Every once in a while I swore I could hear whispers in the breeze, little snippets of icy voices. Sam said she couldn't hear anything. I kept telling myself it was just the wind, but I still felt like we were being watched. Something was out there in the deeper

170

shadows.

After about an hour we finally came to a massive fallen tree, the trunk almost as tall as I was. In the snow-white moonlight I could see that the tree was mottled with moss and lichen; all sorts of creepy crawly bugs probably lived in the rotted wood.

It turns out only one did.

And what a bug it was.

From a small hole in the stump two long legs reached out into the moonlight, like two bony fingers. The spider slowly raised itself out of the hole, its huge black eyes fixing right on me.

It was the most terrifying thing I had ever seen. The eyes seemed to glimmer in the light like black gems, so bulbous they looked like they were about to burst. The brown spider was completely hairless and had a hump on its back, and its legs were impossibly long, twitching with every step. Worst of all, it had two fangs jutting nastily out of its mouth.

"The boy has come," the spider said in a hungry-sounding voice. "We finally meet. The boy who can hear. Two creatures so far from their natural place in the world."

I wasn't about to let my fear get the better of me.

"Nice to meet you," I said. I almost stuck out my hand for a handshake out of habit, but I held back. Spiders probably don't like seeing a human hand reaching for them. That's a good way to get an up close look at those fangs.

"Oh the pleasure is all mine, believe me. My name is Barry."

Okay, his name was less scary than the rest of him, but he was still terrifying.

He sighed, turning those black eyes to the moon thoughtfully. "It is a lonely life, living in solitude so far from home. But one learns a thing or two in years alone. Patience, for one. But most importantly one comes to appreciate what one has lost. And wishes to lose no more."

He snapped those eyes back on me so fast I almost jumped. I didn't know what his game was, but I didn't like it.

"I've had plenty of gibberish the past few days, thanks. Can you help us?"

He sighed again. "I understand your frustration, and your caution. But I am not toying with you. I'm trying to help, in the only way an old spider knows how. I must take my own pace."

I felt bad. "Sorry. I- I thought you were just being difficult."

He sounded amused, like he would have been smirking. You know, if he didn't have fangs instead of a face. "Plenty of difficulty ahead, I'm afraid. But you won't find any here. I have felt the darkness coming, heard the same whispers my brothers have. And I don't wish for my life to change any more than it already has. This wood has become my home, and I will not have it ripped from me in my old age. Please, tell me how I may be of service."

I pulled out the ID card and laid it on the tree trunk. I didn't care for the wet, slimy feel of the rotten wood, but I kept that to myself.

He was fond of his home, after all. To each his own.

"Do you need a light?" I asked, reaching for my flashlight.

"No, thank you just the same. These eyes are not just for show, though they are certainly for that as well," he chuckled.

The spider crawled onto the card. I braced myself. Here was the moment of truth. He started to speak, and I knew, just *knew* he was going to say "Guster Cooper Liberman."

He didn't.

"Easy enough. It says 'Grant County Library.' A simple library card, it would seem."

I was dumbfounded. I could see Sam was too. All this time we had assumed the card was the key to everything, that it would unravel this whole web of mysteries. It seemed it was just another dead end.

"A library card? That's it?"

"So it would seem. There's more however. Fine print. Tiny."

"What does it say?" I held my breath in anticipation.

"It says 'Special Librarian Access.'"

I stared dumbly at him.

A librarian? What librarian? Guster wasn't a librarian. He could barely read.

"It's coming back to me now," William said. "The name. We tried to give you the name of the Masked Marauder the first night we visited you. Did you not receive the message?"

"All I got was instructions to go to Baskertonn Manor, and some numbers."

"Numbers? What numbers?"

I turned to Sam. She had a much better memory than I did.

"They were 2 1 18 19 20 15 14."

William turned around slowly and slapped one of the other spiders upside the head with his leg.

"Jeez Frank! I keep telling you, letters are on the right, numbers on the left. He's got the brain of a fly, that one. Look, we've been referring back to that book to learn your letters. But *some* of us," all eight of his eyes glanced at Frank, "just can't seem to get the hang of it. Sorry about that."

"Wait, what?"

"The alphabet book. Frank was in charge of spelling the name. And he used the numbers instead of the letters."

"Sorry boss," he said, glancing up at me embarrassed.

"Oh, it's okay. You just might have caused the fall of civilization as we know it. Simple mistake." William smacked him upside the head again.

"So what do those letters come out to?" I asked, starting to count through the alphabet.

Once again, Sam was way faster. "B-A-R-S-T-O-N."

Chapter 32
GETTING HELP

There I went again. My mouth was hanging open so wide a crow could have made its nest in there. That's a ridiculous metaphor, of course. There were no birds around.

"Mr. Barston?!"

"That's the one," William said. "A certain Ken Barston. County librarian I believe. The Masked Marauder."

I couldn't believe it. I just couldn't believe it.

"He always seemed so nice, like he wouldn't hurt a fly," Sam said.

"Maybe he wouldn't," William answered. "But he'd apparently hurt Nate's parents."

"Yeah, and we hurt flies, but we're okay," Frank responded.

William smacked him again. "Hardly the point."

I tried to compose myself. We had to move quickly, and this was no time for me to be out of commission with shock. I could detangle the mess in my head later.

"So where do we go from here?"

"Not Baskertonn Manor, I'm assuming," Sam said, turning to William. "I'm sure we left enough signs of our visit there that he wouldn't risk returning."

"Quite right," William responded. "We haven't seen any movement around that place since we came out here. We may not have Barry's eyes, but we're sharp enough."

I asked again. "So where do we go from here?"

"The library?" Sam asked. "I mean, we know who we're after now."

"That's a good idea," I responded. "But it's Sunday. The library's closed, and I don't know how to pick a lock."

"You're not alone anymore," Sam said. "I'm sure one of our animal friends can help get us in."

"Of course we can," Basset said. "I'm not an expert at breaking and entering, but I'm sure we can figure a way in."

"Then it's settled," Sam said. "We're another step closer to getting your parents back, Nate. Don't worry. We're closer."

We started walking back through the dark woods towards downtown.

"So who can help us out?" I asked.

"The squirrels?" Sam responded. "They can climb in through the window or slip in through a crack and unlock the door?"

Basset made a high-pitched whining noise and looked at me like his tail had gotten stepped on.

"Maybe we should hold off on the squirrels," I laughed. "I think we might have used up all the help they're willing to give for a long while."

Sam nodded. "Okay then. What about the spiders?"

"We could get in easy enough," William said. "Then I suppose we could rig up a pulley system made out of webs. Could have that door open in 20 hours or so."

"Yeah, that's not gonna work," I said. "There's not a ton of animals with thumbs. Getting that door open is gonna be a challenge and a half."

"There's a chimp down at the county zoo, but it'd be just as hard to break him out as it will be to break into the library," Sam said. "Who else could turn a doorknob?"

"I have an idea," I said. "It's kind of crazy, but it might just work. Let's go."

I didn't want to say it out loud, not yet. Saying it out loud they might laugh at me, or think I had gone insane with worry for my parents.

I led the group a little further east than we were originally heading, but we were still going in the general direction of downtown.

Just as the sun peeked its head over the horizon, we came to a small, muddy, swampy pond. The sun made the lily pads glisten like emeralds.

Basset and Sam both looked at me with confused faces.

"A fish?" Frank the spider asked. "Are we here for a fish?"

"Yeah, obviously," I responded. "I'm gonna toss a salmon in through the library window and have him splash the door open."

I'd have slapped him upside the head like William, but that would've killed him. Didn't want to do that.

I liked Frank.

I bent down onto my hands and knees, looking straight into a log that was halfway in the water.

"C'mon out," I said quietly. "I know you're awake and can hear us. No point in hiding."

I heard a plop, then a lot of heavy breathing, then anther plop, and finally Gerald the bullfrog came into view from inside the log.

"Good morning boys," Gerald said in his usual tone, like a raspy grandfather who's in the World Series of the Slow-Talking League. Which I really hope isn't a thing. "What can I do for you this morning?"

Still kind of embarrassed by my idea, I bent down and whispered something to Gerald.

Frogs have extremely wide, bulging eyes all the time, so if you've never seen one surprised it's a shocking sight. Gerald opened his eyes so wide it looked like they were about to shoot out of his head with a pop like two grapes being spat out of your mouth.

"Can you do it?" I asked.

"Well, I suppose." Goodness, it was going to take forever just to get an answer from him. Maybe it would have been faster to build that pulley-web system. "I could. But it sounds exhausting."

"Come on. You could do with a bit of exercise. You're getting a little flabby around the middle."

"And around the edges," Sam laughed.

"Thank you," Gerald responded. "We frogs take that as a compliment. Who wants to be skinny as a stick? Must be freezing."

"Look, that's not the point."

"Well then what is? You want to see an old frog make a fool of himself and tucker himself out for your amusement?"

"His parents were kidnapped," Basset said. "This is the only way to get them back."

"Well then what are we waiting for?" Gerald said surprisingly quickly. "Let us make haste. To the library, as fast as we can."

Then he hopped once.

I was a little surprised at how little convincing he needed, but he was a good-hearted frog, and good-hearted people (or animals) need very little convincing to help when something important is on the line. Like kidnapped parents.

He hopped again, then stopped, wheezing.

"And away we go," he said, hopping once more. More

wheezing.

"And again," another hop and another wheeze-pause.

"Phew, we are making *great* time," he said. "Be there by Wednesday at this rate!"

I rolled my eyes, and both Sam and Basset snickered.

I bent down and snatched Gerald off the ground.

"Hey now! Get your hands off me boy! This is extremely impolite! How would you like a giant to grab you and swing you around at a thousand miles per hour? I'm going to be sick. Unhand me boy!"

"Oh relax," I responded.

"Certainly, you can say that now! But I'm about to hurl a load of half-digested flies up onto your hand."

Gross.

"Don't you dare," I responded. "You behave and my friends the spiders will give you all the flies you can eat."

"We will?" Frank asked. That got him another good smack on the head from William. He kept quiet.

"How can I think about food at a time like this?" Gerald sounded really sick.

"I said all the flies you can eat."

He suddenly stopped. I knew he had been faking. "Well then what are we waiting for? Away we go! Mush giant! Mush!"

And away we went.

Chapter 33
SNEAKING IN

We made it to the library about a half-hour after sunrise (which, by the way, was a lot earlier than Wednesday). We snuck around to the back entrance and I put Gerald down on the top step.

He looked up above the door, where a small glass window (I think they call them "transom windows") was cracked open.

"You really expect me to be able to do this?" Gerald asked. He sounded like he just wanted to sleep.

"Of course I do. You're quite talented."

"I can't disagree with you there," he said, puffing out his chest.

After his chest deflated, he looked doubtful again.

"All. The flies. You. Can. Eat." Sam reminded him.

"Right. Well, cheerio. Up, up, and away!"

Gerald's tongue flew out of his mouth at the speed of light, and with a loud snap it stuck to the door knob.

"What the-" Sam started, but before she could finish Gerald sucked his tongue back into his mouth just as fast as he'd struck at the handle. His fat blob of a body whipped up towards the handle, and just before he reached it he released his grip. His body kept spinning upwards past the knob like a green Frisbee made of fat.

Just before he could start falling back down, he snapped his tongue out again, this time at the top of the window.

Bullseye!

He sucked himself up again, and plopped down on the windowsill.

"Gerald, bullfrog acrobat extraordinaire, at your service," he said with a flourish and a bow. "Now, to complete my trick," and he hopped down and out of sight. From inside we could hear a loud splat.

"Ouch! Not to worry. Old Gerald is a lot better than that sounded."

We heard another snap and a sticky ping from the doorknob. Then it turned on its own, and I grabbed it.

I swung the door outwards, and almost got smacked in the face by a swinging Gerald, whose tongue was still stuck to the doorknob. He quickly let go and landed on my shoulder.

"Goodness boy, could've warned me you were going to open the door," he laughed.

"See, I knew this would be fun," I said. Basset and Sam were both staring at me with mouths gaping open and eyes wide with disbelief.

"I can't really deny that," he said. "Might have to make tumbling through the air a regular part of my life. Imagine the excitement in the life of a cat burglar. A bullfrog-burglar; that will become the new name!"

"What will your wife think of that?" I asked with a laugh.

"She can join me! Husband and wife acrobats are all the rage, I'm sure."

I was glad this plan had worked. It would have seemed awfully ridiculous if it had failed. In fact, it seemed awfully ridiculous even when it succeeded.

Gerald stuck out his tongue slightly, with a look of distaste. "Doorknobs are filthy though."

"Yeah, and flies are *so* clean," I laughed.

Gerald winked one bulbous eye at me.

"Well, time to explore! Let us away!"

Gerald clearly had a newfound energy coursing through his body. Excitement can do that. I was sure he'd be sore tomorrow.

He leapt from my shoulder and landed right on Basset's back, grabbing hold of the collar like a horse's reigns.

"Oh come on," Basset said, looking up at me with a disappointed, longsuffering look.

"He can't weigh that much!" Sam laughed.

"Fine. Just as long as none of the female goldens see me," he said, quickly looking around the parking lot.

"I doubt there's a lot of golden retrievers hanging around the empty library," I said.

"Good point." Basset sighed. "Got a good grip there, Gerald?"

"Comfy as a frog on a log," he guffawed. "Or a frog on a dog, as the case may be." He was having too much fun with this.

We walked in through the door, and when it swung shut we were alone in the darkened library.

Chapter 34
THE FINAL CLUES

The bookcases towered over us, casting all the aisles into deeper shadows. The place smelled like musty books and old ink, a smell I usually liked, but today reminded me of a grave.

We crept up to the librarian's desk. It was littered with standard librarian gear: a stack of books to be put away, a few overdue book notices, and a line of dated ink stamps.

I opened the top drawer of the desk, which was full of pens and paper and more stamps.

The second drawer contained a small black appointment book.

I grabbed it and opened it on the desk. I highly doubted he would write down appointments for all of his robberies, but you never know.

The first few pages just said things like "Monday, 12:30, lunch with Pete," and "Friday, 1:45, pick up dry cleaning." Boring stuff.

The fifth page, though, had an entry that said "Saturday, midnight: rob pet store."

Seriously?

"He's no criminal mastermind, that one," Sam said looking over my shoulder.

"He wrote down his crimes in a notebook and left it in his desk?" I asked, incredulous.

"Okay, maybe we're not up against a 'great darkness,'" Sam laughed. "More like a 'slight dimming.' Should we just bring this to the cops?"

"Yes," Basset said without hesitation.

"I don't know," I said. "What if he hurts my parents?"

"How could anyone who leaves evidence like this lying around have eyes and ears everywhere?" Sam asked.

"How could someone like that kidnap my parents in the first place? Something's not right here, and I don't want to risk my parents' safety."

Sam nodded. "You're right."

We kept flipping through the book. There were more normal entries ("Saturday, 7 p.m., dinner with mom"), and here and there more appointments for crimes.

The one from two days ago said "10 a.m. - Nate is on to me. Brought my library access card in to me. He couldn't read it, but poking nose into things."

The next entry said "4 p.m. – kidnapped Nate's parents. Taking them to the picnic area by Nightmare Lake, as instructed."

"There we go!" I shouted. "We know where they are! Let's go."

"Hold on a second," Sam said. "It says 'as instructed.' He's not working alone."

I paused.

"We'll head down to the lake alright, but we can't just rush down there like a herd of elephants," she continued. "If he's not alone, we could be in for a fight. We have to take it slow, sneak up on the lake, and scout it out."

I turned to William. "Can you and your boys take a look down at the lake?"

"I'm afraid not," he said. He looked scared. "We don't go into that part of the woods."

"What? Why not?"

"We just don't. Please, do not ask any more. We don't like to even talk about it. It is too horrific to even think about."

I turned to Sam. "You're right. I think we do need to be careful."

Chapter 35

NIGHTMARE LAKE

We quickly headed back into the woods, thanked the spiders for all their help, and made our way towards the lake.

A place named Nightmare Lake might not sound like the best place for a picnic area, with that cheery name and all, but the politicians opened one there about 50 years ago.

The lake is calm and deep, the perfect place for a swim. The Native Americans named it "Nightmare Lake" because they believed it was haunted by evil spirits and tricksters, but the politicians called that "primitive superstition" and built a picnic and swimming area at the lake anyway.

It didn't go well. Three rowboats sank in the lake the first year, and though no one was hurt, the boats were never found again.

Then the next year four kids almost drowned in the lake. Again no one was seriously hurt, but the kids terrified everyone in town. All four of them said they felt like a rope had tightened around their legs and was trying to drag them down into the black depths of the lake. It was only at the last second that the rope loosened and let them go.

The politicians called it "childhood hogwash," but the

villagers weren't having it.

Just like the Native Americans, people in Grant County started to believe the lake was haunted. Over the past 50 years the picnic area had fallen into disrepair, the benches and tables sagging with age.

I'd been there once when I was exploring (my dad didn't believe in hauntings, so he let me go). I was a little nervous to go swimming in a lake alone (not because it was haunted, of course), so I just poked around. There were some rocks with strange drawings on them, but nothing else that interesting.

As we walked, Gerald bouncing up and down on Basset's back and jiggling with every step, Sam turned to me, a concerned look on her face.

"Look, I don't want to scare you, but I think we're up against something pretty serious here," she said.

"What do you mean? Mr. Barston doesn't seem like the type of person who'd want to hurt anyone, and even if he *did* want to, he doesn't seem like the type of person who *could*."

"He's not alone, remember? And I have an idea of who we're up against."

"Who?" I was shocked she hadn't mentioned anything earlier.

"You really weren't paying attention in Mr. Grimley's history class, were you?"

"What has that got to do with anything? And why *were* you paying attention? No one pays attention."

She blushed.

"Ohhhh, you've got a little crush on him." I patted her on the back. "It's okay. Happens to the best of us." That didn't seem to help much. "So why does it matter?"

"Greek mythology? Athena? The Lakota Indian tribe? You don't remember any of it?"

"Not really." I still didn't see where this was going.

"Like I said, I don't want to scare you, so I'm going to keep my theories to myself for now. Just keep your eyes open. If I'm right, we'll really need to be on the lookout."

She was doing the exact opposite of not scaring me. She was freaking me out. I looked up into the branches of the trees and into every shadow and behind every rock as we walked, but I didn't notice anything unusual.

I turned and looked at Basset. My hands were shaking and my palms were all sweaty from the nerves. I felt like I was about to go on a roller coaster.

You know, if a roller coaster wanted to kill me and my parents.

"I have to admit, I'm a little scared," I said.

"Me too," Sam whispered.

"It's embarrassing, but I can't stop being afraid. What if we mess up? What if we get hurt, or worse, if my parents get hurt? I wish I had more courage."

Basset stopped and looked me right in the eyes.

"True courage doesn't mean you're not afraid," he said. "It means that doing the right thing outweighs your fears. True courage is selfless."

I wasn't sure what to say.

"Listen," he continued. "Porcupines aren't good playmates, but a lot of dogs still poke their noses into porcupine holes. Ignoring the fear of porcupines isn't brave, it's stupid. But if another dog needs to be protected from a porcupine, *that's* when you push past the fear. True courage isn't ignoring your fear for no reason. True courage is putting someone else ahead of yourself, even if you're afraid. That's what we're doing today."

Sam straightened her shoulders.

"We're going to rescue your parents," she said. "And the

whole town. That's worth the risk."

I nodded back.

"We can do this. Together."

Around noon we came to the old dirt road that led up to the picnic area. The path was choked with weeds and brush, and even some smaller trees, but you could tell it used to be a popular road. The ruts were still deep, and a few rusty signs still waved in the wind.

"Okay, the picnic area is just around that corner up there, right?" I pointed ahead to where the road curved to the left. Sam nodded. "So let's cut through the woods here quietly. The bushes around the clearing are thick, so we should be able to peek out without anyone seeing us coming."

"Sounds like a plan," Sam said. "You sure you're with us in this?" Sam asked, turning to Gerald.

"For sure, young lady! I have discovered a new outlook on life, it would seem. A grand outlook. Adventure: that's the name of the game now. Come!" He lifted Basset's collar like reigns and tapped him on the sides. "Yah! On Lassie!"

"It's Basset," my dog said, still pretty glum about being made into a horse.

"Just having a bit of fun, old chum. I've never seen you so down in the dumps before. Adventures are grand, are they not? Chin up, come on!"

"Any chance you could sneak through the woods and see what we're up against?" I asked him.

"I said I had a new outlook on life, not a new set of legs. It'd still take me a few hours to make it there, I'm afraid."

"Fair enough," I said with a laugh. "Fair enough."

We crept through the woods until the tall bushes that surrounded the picnic area were right in front of us.

My hands were drenched in cold sweat, and my stomach

was doing back flips. Who knew what was beyond those bushes? Who knew if my parents were okay, or if an army of monsters waited ahead of us?

I bent down onto my knees and carefully, slowly, ever so slowly, parted the branches of the bush.

I was convinced I was making too much noise. My breathing sounded impossibly loud in my ears, and my heart was pounding as hard as a drum. The leaves rustled no matter how hard I tried to move slowly, but I kept telling myself that the woods always rustle and make noise. No one would think this was odd.

I peered through the branches, and at first everything seemed just fine.

Mr. Barston had his back to me, and was looking down at one of the sagging picnic tables, where a few crumbling Native American relics were piled up.

I looked around the clearing, and didn't see anything else. It looked like our enemy was alone.

Then I remembered Sam's advice. And it's a good thing I did.

I glanced up into the trees above Mr. Barston, not really expecting to see anything, and my breath caught in my throat.

My parents were hanging from the trees.

They looked alright. They were definitely breathing. But they were unconscious, wrapped up tight in white silk and dangling from the branches.

That wasn't even the worst of it.

The entire tree canopy was covered in a maze of spider webs, with thousands upon thousands of huge, furry spiders scurrying all over their network.

Chapter 36

TRAPPED

This was why William and his tribe wouldn't come anywhere near here. They were outnumbered 10 to 1.

Sam was crouching right next to me, looking up at the webs with a calm look on her face.

"This is what I was afraid of," she said. "Spiders."

"How could you know?" I whispered back.

"Athena. In Greek legend, she turned one of her servants into a spider during a tapestry-weaving contest. Athena is the mother of spiders."

"Well that's a silly story."

"Oh, definitely. But everything in Baskertonn Manor, everything, had to do with Athena. And then when William said they wouldn't come here, I remembered that little snippet from class, and I put the two together. Why else would William be so terrified of this place?"

I was about to ask why the people in Baskertonn Manor would be so obsessed with spiders, but I didn't get the chance. I got a shiver, and felt like a cloud had drifted in front of the sun. It had certainly gotten darker.

I looked up, and nearly peed my pants. Seriously.

These spiders were fast. The trees above us were now full

of webs, blocking out a good amount of light. And they were now descending towards us, building a wall to block us in. They were about 100 yards behind us. At the rate they were moving, we'd never get there before the wall was finished. And it looked *strong*.

But Basset was a lot faster than us.

"Basset, buddy, I need you to run as fast as you can and get past that wall," I whispered urgently.

"I'm not leaving you. Not ever, and especially not at a time like this."

"It might be our only chance. I need you to get away and see if you can find another way back to us. See if you can get the drop on these guys."

"I'm not leaving."

"It's the only way," Sam said, scratching behind his ears. "I'll look after him while you're gone. Promise."

Basset looked doubtful.

"Come, old buddy," Gerald said. "Surprise attack, that's the game now. We'll come back for them forthwith."

Basset licked my hand. "Don't do anything dangerous."

"I think we're already neck deep in dangerous," I laughed. "I'll be alright. Now go!"

He gave me one last look, but knew there was no more time. He bolted straight back into the woods, like a streak of gold lightning. Gerald was bouncing so hard on his back I thought he might pop, but the little guy held on tight.

I looked up above, where the spiders were busily expanding their web. Some of them looked almost as big as a small dog, which I was almost sure was impossible. There *aren't* any spiders that big. But when you see it with your own eyes it's hard to argue.

Spiders. I was done with spiders.

The spiders knew we were here, but Mr. Barston didn't. It

was time to find out what this was all about.

If you can't fight your way out of something you might as well try to talk your way out.

I was shaking inside, but hey, fake it 'til you make it, right?

Sam and I walked straight through the bushes.

Chapter 37
FACE TO FACE WITH THE ENEMY

"Kind of a dim afternoon, isn't it?" I said casually with my hands in my pockets.

Mr. Barston whirled around so fast he almost knocked one of the Native American artifacts off the table. There was a look of shock on his face that quickly changed into a look of arrogant contempt. More prideful than Genevieve, more disgusted at our presence than the squirrels at the sight of Basset.

"Finally found me, eh boy?" he said, rolling his eyes. "Took you long enough. And now you're stupid enough to walk right into the spider's web."

He walked towards me and motioned to the treetops.

"Look around you. Your parents are in the palm of my hand, and now so are you."

"Doesn't look like it's *your* palm I'm dealing with, actually," I said calmly, looking up at the trees as well. "I'm assuming you work for them."

"They work for me," he said, tapping himself on the chest.

"I hope you're right. We're not the only ones in the middle of this web."

He looked uncomfortable for a second. I don't think he'd realized that yet. No criminal mastermind for sure, but he quickly composed himself.

"How *did* you find me?"

I pulled out the calendar. "You're new to this life of crime, huh?"

His eyes grew wide with surprise, but he lied right through his teeth. "I wanted you to find that. Fell for my trap."

"Yeah, guess we did," Sam said. "Fell right into it. Smack!"

"You're awfully calm about it," he responded.

"Well, it's obvious we lost," I said. "No point in crying over spilled milk, is there? Why fight it if it's so obvious?"

Our calmness was really starting to shake him. He expected us to be quivering in our sneakers.

"What's going on here?"

Sam straightened up to her full height, towering over the spindly little man.

"Why don't *you* tell *us*," she said. "We're about to be eaten by a bunch of spiders, right? Might as well explain all this."

"Can't do any harm, I suppose," he said pridefully, though he was clearly terrified of Sam. He turned back to look at his Native American artifacts. "I'm guessing you children are too stupid to have figured it out by now."

"What, you're planning on taking over the world with a few spiders?" I asked. "I think tanks and bombs and guns versus spiders isn't really much of a fight."

"Oh, it's so much more than that, boy," he said, his eyes getting a disturbing sparkle as he looked at the relics. "So much more. My family has been working on forging a connection with the animal world for generations. We didn't have much success…until now."

"Your family?" I asked.

He sighed. "The townspeople didn't take well to what they called our 'kooky beliefs' and chased us out of our manor. Over time, more and more in my family came to agree with them, until I was the only descendent left who believed in the old ways. I decided to come back here, an outcast from my own family and from the village that was rightfully ours."

"You're a Baskertonn?"

"You really are slow, aren't you? I couldn't very well return under my family's name, so I changed it. But I still wanted to honor my ancestors, so I kept all the letters. Ken Barston: rearrange it a little, and you get Baskertonn. Simplest thing."

I was shocked, but for once I kept my mouth from hanging open. I wasn't going to show him my surprise.

"What do you mean you've been successful?"

"Haven't you noticed? Those spiders up there, some of them are as large as a dog. I've found a way to make them grow, not just in size but in intelligence and in speed, and in sheer ferocity. They cannot speak to me, but they understand me now. Years of talking to them and finally, *finally* they can understand me." He looked like he was trying to appear terrifying, but just like the painting in Baskertonn Manor he looked like a kid on Halloween: someone weak trying to act scary. And failing.

Sam, on the other hand, didn't even have to try. She took another step toward Mr. Barston. Mr. Baskertonn. Whatever.

"So you have a race of super-spiders. So what?"

"That's only the beginning. There's so much more I can do. But even now, even this is dangerous enough. Think about it: who would suspect this? Who thinks anything of insects, other than as pests? No one will know there's something going on until it's too late."

He was clearly mad: spiders aren't insects.

They're arachnids.

He had a point though. It was crazy, but it was a point. *You* try telling the army there's a conspiracy of super-spiders bent on taking over the world. I don't think that'd get you much further than a padded cell.

We had to stop him. First step: keep him talking long enough for Basset to find a way to help us. Getting him to talk wasn't going to be hard: this kook was clearly proud of his plan.

"Okay, so now we know what you're doing, and why. But how?" I tried to sound impressed at his mind-shatteringly crazy ideas instead of laughing at them. "How did you do it?"

"Don't you know anything?" He motioned to the artifacts on the table. "The Lakota tribe feared the spiders, saw them as tricksters and evil creatures."

"Shoot. I guess I wasn't paying attention in my 'Spider-Worshiping Ancient Cultures' class again."

"Don't be snide with me boy."

"Me? Snide? Never! I don't even know what the word means? Is it some sort of slide made out of snow? Snow-slide. Snide? Then again, I don't see why you'd call me a snow-slide, so that's probably not it…"

He cut me off.

"Using their artifacts in one of their unholy places, I was able to communicate with the spiders, and eventually control them."

"Ohhh, that makes sense," Sam said, twirling her finger around her ear while looking at me, as if to say "nut job."

"Look around you child! It worked, did it not?"

"Yes," I said. "Congratulations. You've created slightly larger spiders. The world trembles at the sound of your voice."

"It will," he said.

It did actually explain some things. With an army of spiders, we finally knew how he could steal so many items in such a short amount of time. That's a lot of helping hands. And now we knew why he wanted to get rid of the birds: they eat spiders.

"But why did you steal from those other stores? I get the Lakota exhibit, but why comics and lumber and pet supplies?"

"The pet shop provided me with cages. When my spiders get large enough they will need more than bugs to feed on. The neighborhood pets will do nicely."

I grimaced.

"The lumber is to help me fix up my family manor and turn it into the palace it should rightfully be."

"And comics?"

"I thought the spiders might like to read a bit about Spiderman." He turned and looked at a stack of shredded, brightly colored paper that was covered in spider spit. "I was wrong on that one."

He was more than nuts. He was batty, daffy, crackers. He was a flock of bats watching Daffy Duck cartoons while eating an entire grocery store full of nuts and crackers.

After that simile, I'm starting to think it was wearing off on me.

"I'm tired of talking," Mr. Baskertonn said, snapping his fingers.

I looked up and saw at least 50 fat, hairy spiders sliding down their silken strings towards us.

Time for one last show of fake-bravery.

"Alright Baskertonn. Times up," I said. "You don't think we would've come in here without backup, do you?"

"What, you mean that mongrel and his pet frog?" Mr. Baskertonn laughed. "I sent my spiders after them. Your dog's not as fast as you think he is. He's failed you, I'm afraid."

Okay, now I was scared.

The spiders up above were clicking their fangs together, and making a terrible squelching sound as they descended towards our faces.

And we were surrounded.
There was no way out.

Chapter 38
THE FIGHT BEGINS

"Failed? Basset has never failed anyone, not in his life, and he's not about to fail now!" I heard a voice ring out from the treetops. "You cannot hope to escape from –" there was a pause, and then I saw a green blur whizzing through the air. It smacked straight into five of the spiders, sending them sailing and splatting into a tree trunk, then it landed in a pile of leaves.

"Basset and His Amazing Acrobatic Amphibian!" Gerald leapt from the leaves. "Name's a work in progress."

The remaining spiders changed course and started clambering for Gerald, but at that moment I saw the greatest sight I've ever seen in my entire life: Basset came charging out of the woods, barreling straight for Mr. Baskertonn.

Before the man could even turn around, Basset chomped down hard on his rear end.

"Yow!" Mr. Barston screamed as he jumped and ran into the woods. "Ow, ow, ow!"

Basset came running up to me, and Sam and I rushed over and wrapped our arms around him.

"Blech! Crazy-man butt tastes awful," he said. Then he got serious. "I'd never fail you buddy."

"I know boy, I know," I said, tightening my hug. "And I'd

200

never fail you."

"I hate to break up this touching moment, but we're far from out of the woods, if you'll pardon the expression," Gerald said, hopping over to us.

I looked up. Mr. Baskertonn had been chomped, but he wasn't out of commission. I saw him limping back towards us, and up above, thousands of spiders were assembling for an attack.

And there were only four of us.

All of the biggest spiders were on their way down, the ones the size of a cat or larger.

They spat out a horrible hissing, gnashing noise as they descended, a few of them spitting out bits of web onto us to taunt us.

It was sticky and gross, but not very effective.

The smaller spiders stayed up in the web, cheering their big brothers on, probably because it would have been so easy for them to get squished. I don't think they knew how easily frightened we are of spiders, even if we can easily squish them.

"What do we do now?" I asked, jerking my head from side to side to see if there was a way out. There wasn't. The huge spiders were all around us, and the web wall was now complete.

"I'm glad you came back for us and all, but it looks like you just postponed our deaths by a few seconds," Sam said.

"And gave the spiders more flavor options to choose from," I added.

"I couldn't leave you here alone, even if I knew I'd die," Basset said, holding his head high and licking my hand. "We can fight them off as long as we can."

"Certainly my boy," Gerald nodded.

Mr. Baskertonn had finally regained his composure, and was watching the spiders descend with hungry eyes.

"Their first taste of true battle," he hissed. "I think they'll get a craving for it."

The lowest spider was just feet above me now, so close I could see its hairs twitching and its fangs glistening with venom.

Basset and Gerald's grand entrance had given me some hope, but I didn't know what to do now.

Basset barked at the nearest spider, causing it to twitch, but it kept coming at him. Gerald struck at one with his tongue, which made it lose its grip, but it landed on its feet and scuttled right for him.

I rushed over to help, but I heard a plop behind me and quickly felt something sticky wrap its way around my legs.

I looked back, and a 50 pound spider was just inches from my face, my feet wrapped in its web.

Basset growled low in the back of his throat and leapt at the spider. He clamped down hard on one of the spider's legs, snapping it right off. The two animals rolled over in a heap to my left, scuffling and biting at each other.

I got onto my feet, kicked off the web, grabbed a nearby stick, and rushed over to help my dog.

The spider had him pinned, and was just about to sink his fangs into him when I brought the stick down on the furry head.

With a loud crack the spider rolled onto its back, its legs curling up.

Basset got to his feet, and I whirled around to see how Gerald was doing. Sam had gotten to Gerald's side and apparently picked up his attacker and lobbed him at another spider, both of which were now tangled in a pile next to a tree.

Basset and I rushed over next to them. We had dispatched three of our attackers. We were now surrounded by about 30 more.

The circle was slowly closing. They were nervous. They didn't want to be the next to get smacked by my stick or bitten by Basset, but they'd get us eventually.

"I'm sorry it has to end like this, boy," I said to Basset.

My dog looked up into my eyes with that goofy smile. "What do you mean? I'm at your side. Where would I rather it end?"

I almost laughed and cried at the same time.

I was trying to stay brave, but it was a losing battle. I kept imagining how those fangs would feel as they sank into my skin, how it would burn, how long I'd stay conscious before passing out from the pain.

An active imagination can be a curse.

If you've ever been attacked by a dog or faced down a bully, you know how terrifying it can be in the moment, a haze of fear closing in on your vision. But instead of one attacker, I was faced with dozens. And instead of a dog or a bully, it was giant spiders.

We were going to die.

And it was going to be painful.

Chapter 39

DIRE TROUBLE

At that moment I heard a loud tearing noise like a ripping sweater. I turned to face the sound, and saw the web wall separating like it was being cut by a pair of scissors.

I was confused.

The spiders retreated a bit, waiting to see what had torn through their defenses.

Through the rip in the wall a huge shape started barreling towards us like a massive rolling boulder. The spiders all hissed again and backed up further. Whatever it was, it was enormous. And round.

Finally it stopped, just short of a shaft of light.

"Good to see you Bassy," a soft voice purred. "I heard you and your humans got into a spot of trouble, so I did what I do best: I spread the news."

Genevieve stepped into the light, smiling wide at us.

"You didn't think the neighborhood would let you die all alone, did you Bassy?"

The spiders were watching us warily, but I could see in the larger ones' eyes that the sight of a fat cat was quite appetizing. They wouldn't wait long.

"Why would you come from your comfy rock into the

woods to help me?" Basset asked. He sounded downright flabbergasted. "You hate the woods."

"Yes, but I hate seeing my friends hurt even more than I hate this filthy place," she looked, for the first time ever, kind of shy. "Besides . . . you've always been nice to me Basset. Never making fun of my . . . shape. Most animals just want me for my news, but you . . . you're different."

I smiled.

"And I didn't come alone."

Bounding through the rip came an extremely fast, extremely pudgy shadow.

That wazzled.

"Hey guys I heard there was a fight and I could help and I love helping don't I guys I'm good at helping aren't I?" Franklin wagged his tail and rushed up to Sam, licking her hand like it was a popsicle.

A cat the size of a boulder and a puggle are good company, but I wasn't sure how useful they'd be in a fight. The spiders started inching towards us again.

"Oy! Ugly! I've fought spiders as big as a bus and didn't get a scratch. Who do you think you are, picking on me mates?" I almost laughed. Basset really did have some friends.

A pack of 10 weasels – led by good old "Everglade Amsterdam Eustace Chiselbottom Cherith Wonderstone Hummingbird Saltalamacchia" or whatever his name was – scurried into the light.

"Think some spider webs can hold off these teeth?" Everglade said, baring his fangs at the spiders. "Don't think so. These babies can cut through anything, and that ain't even a lie," he winked at me as he pulled up beside me.

"Good to see ya, Basset," he said. "Again, not even a lie. Sometimes honesty's useful. Ain't that what yer always sayin'?"

Basset was practically beaming. Even if we died today, we'd die with friends.

"But we don't have any weapons," Sam said.

"You have our teeth," the weasel said.

"And my claws," Genevieve added.

"And my tongue," Gerald croaked.

"And Franklin's boundless energy," I laughed.

"We can do this, buddy," Basset said, looking straight at me. "Together."

"Now this is more like it lads! A fair fight, that's what we needed," Gerald said. He climbed aboard Basset's back. "Now...CHARGE!"

Basset ran headlong into the crowd of spiders, followed closely by the weasels.

The spiders charged back.

The weasels all piled onto different spiders ten times their size, their teeth sinking deep. I was right to not want to mess with a weasel.

Just as Basset leapt for a spider, Gerald used his tongue to grab a tree branch, swing himself off Basset's back, up into the air, and land right on the spider's eyes.

"The beast is blinded! Strike, Basset, strike!" He shouted. Basset struck, biting the spider's legs and dragging it to the side.

A movie about a talking rhinoceros who does karate to fight some evil penguins might not be very realistic, but I've seen a bullfrog do acrobatic kung fu.

Sam and I rushed into the fray, both carrying heavy sticks.

The next few minutes were a blur. Huge, hairy bodies pushed against me and threw me around, but I always regained my feet. I clubbed and batted at spindly legs and bulbous bodies. I dodged fangs that missed me by inches and did my best to keep the spiders away from Genevieve, who, let's face it, was more useful gathering soldiers than being one.

Gerald kept swinging around by his tongue, leaping from spider to spider and creating quite a bit of disorder. And I don't think Franklin bit a single enemy, but he sure knocked a few off their legs when he bowled them over. He was just running all over the place with his tongue flapping in the breeze and having a good old time.

I couldn't really tell how we were doing over all. Every second I was either striking or defending, but it didn't seem like we were getting anywhere, and I was becoming exhausted. Based on the cheering from up above, it didn't sound like things were going well for us.

I glanced over and saw Basset pinned under the biggest spider I'd seen yet. Sam was stuck fending off three of her own, and the weasels were standing in a tight group with their backs against a boulder, surrounded by a dozen massive tarantulas.

I rushed over to Basset and whacked the spider off him with my stick, which shattered at the impact. I was now weaponless.

I ran to the side of the weasels with Basset and Franklin following close behind.

"Sam! Genevieve! Regroup!" I shouted.

Sam quickly snatched Genevieve up off the ground and raced over to my side.

We were all battered and bloodied and breathing heavily. Another dozen spiders joined the group surrounding us. The cheering up above grew to a feverish pitch.

I heard a cold, maniacal laugh from the trees.

Mr. Baskertonn sat suspended in a seat made of webs, high up in the boughs.

"The coward didn't even join the fight," Basset said.

"You put up quite an entertaining show," Baskertonn said,

still laughing. "But I'm afraid it has to come to an end. I'll have to find more entertainment elsewhere, I suppose."

Suddenly I felt the ground shudder once. Then again. Then yet again. Like a giant was walking through the woods.

I wasn't far off. A spider at least as tall as I was stomped its way into the clearing. It slowly made its way to the circle surrounding us, and all the other spiders backed away in either awe or fear, or maybe both. It looked right at me, and clicked its fangs together twice.

"Well this is unfortunate," I said.

"Quite," Sam responded.

Chapter 40
A SURPRISE APPEARANCE

"No more tricks up your sleeves, eh?" Mr. Baskertonn called from his seat. "No hedgehogs hiding in the woods, or some other cute critters to join you? No?"

"Oh, I wouldn't say we're quite out," I heard Genevieve mutter behind me. "We might have one last trick."

I didn't know what she meant, but I didn't have time to think about it.

The giant spider crouched down like a cat about to spring, and then it leapt through the air.

Sometimes – like when you're falling from high up in a tree or a bully is about to punch you – time seems to go in slow motion. This was one of those times. I could see every hair on that spider's body quiver as it soared through the air. I could see its black eyes lock onto mine. And I could see its fangs, the length of my pointer finger, coming straight for my face.

Just as it was about to strike, something came whistling through the air and whacked it right on the head.

The spider went sailing back and landed in the leaves with a thud.

It quickly scrambled to its feet and came charging again.

Another projectile hit it.

Suddenly a rain of stones or something similar started whizzing out of the trees, plunking down on the heads of the spiders.

Our enemies hissed angrily, but were too slow to avoid getting hit again and again.

I looked up in the trees, confused.

"You bugs are lugs," a high pitched voice shouted from above.

"Hairy isn't so scary."

"Quite the contrary."

I looked more closely. The missiles were all acorns.

A squirrel stepped out onto a branch confidently, looking straight down at us.

"Did Basset get himself stuck in another tight spot?"

"Wha- how- but why?" Basset stammered out.

"Well said," came a mocking voice from deeper in the woods.

"Now, now Basset," the squirrel right above us said. "If you were eaten by spiders, who would we have left in the neighborhood to make fun of?"

Basset looked annoyed, but the squirrel winked at me.

"C'mon Basset, don't you know it's all a game?" the squirrel continued. "There's not an animal in the village that doesn't respect you. Now quit sulking and help us get these nasty things out of our forest!"

The hail of nuts and acorns continued to pelt the spiders as the rest of us rushed at them. We pushed them back further and further, until they finally turned and ran.

Up above I heard the sound of thousands of tiny feet scurrying away.

"You haven't seen the last of me!" Mr. Baskertonn shouted from up above.

The web he was sitting on tightened suddenly, wrapping him up completely as he was dragged away. I could hear his muffled cries from inside, but couldn't tell what he was saying.

To this day I'm not sure if he was continuing to taunt us, or if he was calling for help because the spiders had betrayed him.

Either way, it was over.

Chapter 41
PUTTING EVERYTHING BACK TOGETHER

Cleaning up after this mess was relatively easy. We disposed of the dead spiders in the lake, and cleaned up the clearing as best we could.

We decided we didn't want to have to explain where a bunch of mutant spiders had come from.

We cut my parents down, and found them still unconscious.

By that point William's tribe had rejoined us.

"They'll be fine," he said after looking my parents over. "The venom just put them to sleep. They won't remember a thing. They'll be a bit nauseous when they first wake up. Just tell them they had the flu and you took care of them."

The rest of the animals returned home, and Basset, Sam and I soon followed.

"You think this is the last we've seen of those guys?" Sam asked.

"I think so," I said.

"I sure *hope* so," Basset added.

I sighed. "But I get the feeling this isn't the last weird thing that's going to happen. Did you look at those Native American artifacts?"

Sam sighed too. "Yeah, I did."

"They weren't anything interesting, right? No magic incantations or anything?"

"No. Mr. Baskertonn was just a loon. There was nothing special about those things."

"So the spiders started learning how to talk on their own. And they grew huge on their own. Something bigger is going on here. The world is changing."

We got home around sunset and tucked my parents into bed.

Basset and I soon retired to my room as well, with Sam heading home.

As we settled into bed, I turned to Basset.

"Looks like things can get back to normal now," I said. "Well, as normal as life can be for a boy who can hear animals," I laughed. "Like nothing happened."

"But nothing didn't happen," Basset responded. "We've been through something pretty serious here buddy. We'd be stupid not to learn from it. Go to sleep, but I think you'll find that you've grown from all this. We all have."

Basset always gave good advice.

Even before he could talk to me.

He was right. Guster still waited for me when school got back in, but I was hoping I'd learned a thing or two about sticking up for myself. You don't accomplish anything by ignoring problems or running away from them. You enlist the help of friends and figure out a solution.

I'd have to wait and see if I could apply those lessons. It's a lot easier to be brave when you don't have a Brussels-sprout-breathed bully glowering down at you.

But even if my bully problems weren't completely solved, I thought I'd still be alright. I had my parents. I had Basset and Sam and my books. Not everything can go your way in life, after all. You have to put up with the bad by focusing on the good. Change what you can, live with the rest.

I would focus on the squirrels on the ground, and remember Franklin's boundless optimism.

That was my plan, at least.

That was my plan.

THE END

Made in the USA
Middletown, DE
06 May 2016